THE ROAD TO MARIETTA

Karla Jordan

PRAISE FOR KARLA JORDAN'S DEBUT NOVEL, CARTWHEELS IN THE DARK.

"Cartwheels In The Dark is a journey back in time full of unexpected outcomes."-Feathered Quill

"Karla Jordan's debut novel is an emotional story about confronting ones past. The book has an intriguing plot that's part mystery, part women's fiction..."-Annette G. Anders, Author of THE FULL CIRCLE SERIES

"This story pulled at my heart from the beginning to the end of the book." -Net Galley Reviews

AUTHOR'S NOTE

Though this story references historical events, this is a work of fiction. Names, characters, events, dates, and incidents are used fictitiously or are products of my imagination.

ACKNOWLEDGEMENTS

Thank you to my husband, Dana, who selflessly picks up the slack when I am obsessively writing and editing a book. I love you and I couldn't do this without you.

I'd also like to thank my dear friend, Cathe, who once again, spent endless hours of reading the same words repeatedly for months. Your input is appreciated more than you know. You keep me on track and have no problem telling me when I'm being ridiculous, which we both know I desperately need. Thirty years of friendship makes us family now, in my book.

I am also grateful to my grown children, Amanda, Hunter, Nick and Alexie for your love and support of my projects. This book is also for my granddaughter, Erin. Never give up that dream. Hard work always pays off. I love you all more than you could ever know.

A huge THANK YOU to all of you who read my debut novel, "Cartwheels In The Dark" and gave reviews for my work as well as for "The Road to Marietta." I am so grateful and fortunate for all the friends and supporters who have stuck by me through this process and are always "in my corner." Your kindness, generosity and support means the world.

"Thank you" doesn't seem enough. I'll be forever grateful that you gave this "Maine girl" a chance.

Last and by no means, the least, I want to thank my father, Carlton Worthley for always supporting me with this dream and in life in general. He once told me, during a frustrating time of writing, *The finish line is near, you'll get there before you know it.* You were right, Dad. As always. I love you .

CHAPTER ONE

1930 Chicago

August Violet Finnegan spent the better part of her childhood gallivanting around the country with her father, a traveling salesman. At twelve years old, she had practically grown up in the back seat of one car or another. They didn't own much and what they did have fit inside their Model A Ford, one of the finest automobiles that money could buy at the time. Her father never compromised when it came to his car, boasting that a beautiful automobile was a necessity in his line of work.

Once her father made a sale, he would head off to the nearest underground gin joint where he would quickly forget that there was a little girl waiting back in that fancy car. Alone.

August slept in the car. She ate in the car. She washed herself as best as she could in gas station restrooms that were filthy and smelly. That was her life, every single day. They were always on the road heading somewhere and nowhere at the same time it seemed.

He didn't want to be her father and told her so at least once every day for as long as she could remember. "If the good Lord had only seen fit to give me at *least* half a brain, I'd have driven to the nearest orphanage and left you there years ago" was one of his favorite rants. It was also how he got her to behave on those long, monotonous road trips between cities. The threat of living at an orphanage hung over her head every minute of every day. If she had a penny or even half of that, for the times she'd heard him say how he hated to open his eyes and see her face every morning, she'd have been a rich little girl.

Without trying, August had a knack for upsetting her father. When she was younger but old enough to ask him questions that he didn't want to answer, he got very agitated. One time he was so angry with her that he drove her straight to the closest children's home. He'd dragged her inside a tall, square brick building that smelled of both mold and cleaning oil.

They walked down a long hallway that seemed

to go on forever, with rooms on either side. Some doors were open, though most were not. Every door had a small window through which August could see children inside. They didn't look like any kids she'd ever seen before. Anywhere.

It was hard to tell them apart with their shaved heads and matching tattered grey nightshirts. Each room had six small beds, and more than a dozen children per room. Pin striped mattresses were thin, stained, and soiled. There hadn't even been blankets or sheets on any of the beds.

The children were filthy, and she could smell the most gut-wrenching odors filling the air. Peeking into one room, she saw a boy, at least she thought it was a boy, painting on the wall. She realized as she watched that it was not a drawing made with crayons or pencils but with blood. Fresh blood, trickling out of his own finger and smeared on the wall.

As they walked further down the hall, there were sounds of terrifying screams and heartbreaking cries echoing in the distance like she'd never heard before and hoped to never again hear. August still remembered how she grabbed her father's hand and begged him to take her outside. He didn't seem to care that she was horrified.

"You stand right here a bit longer and get a good look-see. You take this all in and make damn sure you never forget what you're seeing, girl." he barked at her.

"Why Daddy? I don't want to see this. I'm scared! I want to leave, Daddy!"

August was seven years old at the time and

terrified beyond anything she ever thought possible.

"You paint a picture in your mind of what you are seeing here, girl. Paint that picture *good*. This is where you could be living. *Could be* and *will be* if I can't make you mind. A place just like this is where your Mama grew up and promise or no promise, you do as I say or so help me, I'll drop you off at the nearest one of these places that I can find. I swear I'll drive away and leave you right there."

She remembered how she shook and cried uncontrollably. Her father bent down to her eye level and said, "I ain't having none of that crying business. I'm a man who has no use for any of those shenanigans. Do you hear me? You'd *better* hear me, or I promise you, you'll find yourself sharing a room with one of these kids right here!"

August could feel with every bone in her body that he meant what he said. As much as her chest felt like she could have cried a bucket full or two, she swallowed every tear so he wouldn't see a single one fall down her cheeks. She understood right then that she'd have to always do her best to never make him angry enough to bring her to a place like that and leave her behind.

Not even when she was so hungry that her stomach growled out loud. Not even when she had to pee so bad she thought she would explode. No. She'd learned quite well how to keep to herself and hardly let him know she was even there in that backseat.

August tried to bury the truth way down deep where she could pretend it didn't exist, but it wasn't working. She and her father both knew the truth. He didn't want her around and never had. She was a liability he didn't want to deal with. As long as she was quiet for hours on end amusing herself with reading or sleeping, he was happy. When it was dinnertime, he'd toss a sandwich into the back seat for her. When he was tired, he'd park somewhere, and they would sleep. In the meantime, any little peep out of her was as he told her quite often, "a goddamned burden he didn't need and never wanted."

The only reason she was with him at all was because he'd made a promise to her mother, who died shortly after giving birth. He promised his wife that her precious daughter would be well taken care of and would never be left at an orphanage as she herself had been. He assured her that her daughter wouldn't suffer as she had during her own childhood.

There were countless times that August wished she had a mother. The only thing she really knew about hers was that she had given her the name of August Violet. August for the month she was born in, and Violet after her mother's favorite flower that grew wild and untamed in the Midwest. For the first five years of her life, she hadn't even known her father. He had dropped her off with his sister, Maggie, until August was old enough to travel with him. Shortly after he'd come for her, she found herself wishing that he had never bothered to come back at all.

The way August saw it, her father had kept *half* of his promise to her mother. He was keeping her alive but saying that she was "well taken care of" was a leap.

A big one.

Her aunt Maggie had been a stern, Catholic woman who liked things done to her liking. Everything had to be perfect, which August quickly learned. The utensils were to be shined and laid carefully on top of one another in the drawer, lined up precisely. The beds were to be made so tight that they could have bounced a coin on top of them. Dust was the "Devil's friend," so there could be none of that found anywhere in her home. However, she had taken the time to teach August things a girl her age should know, including how to read. If not for her aunt, she wouldn't know how to read a single word and she knew that. Her life with John Finnegan was about as far from life back in the suburbs of Chicago with Maggie, as one could get.

Not long before the bottom dropped out of her world, she realized what her Daddy was selling as a "salesman." She'd never asked him and never had any interest in what it was that he kept in the back of the car. But one day that all changed. *Everything* changed.

She wished now that she hadn't seen but she had, and he knew that she knew. The big question was what he was going to do about it. His silence was terrifying. Almost worse than getting her backside whacked for misbehaving. Would he really bring her to an orphan's home? Could a man really do that to his only child? She already knew the answer to that question but wished she didn't.

They had stopped for gas at a station somewhere in New Jersey. Her father needed to use the "facilities," as he called it. He woke August up with a slap to her head and told her to pump the gas for him while he was gone.

Apparently, the female clerk with the bright red hair had to use the same "facilities" because her father hadn't been gone ten seconds when she followed him around the corner of the building.

August did as she was told and got out of the car to fill the tank. As she stood pumping gas into the tank, the trunk of the car popped open just a little. She didn't know how it happened, but the latch had come loose. She had never once looked in the trunk nor had she ever been curious to know what was inside. She knew whatever was in there was off limits. Her father had threatened a time or two hundred about ever getting into his business "in the back."

As she looked at that lid, she knew she should push it down tight until she heard it click. That's what she *should* have done. Instead, she reached for the open trunk and barely touched the lid with one finger when the door flew wide open. At that point, it was impossible not to notice the boxes of Mason jars that filled the trunk. Before she had a minute to think about what she was doing, she reached for one of the jars and held it in her hand. It was filled with a clear liquid of some sort. She unscrewed the lid and took a sniff of the water- like fluid inside. It didn't smell like water at all. She realized it didn't smell much different than the gasoline she was pumping into the tank of the car. She knew then it was moonshine liquor because that was the odor she smelled on her father often. How anyone could swallow something that smelled so bad was beyond her, but she'd seen her Daddy and his "associates" drinking from jars just like those, when she was supposed to be asleep.

She could count on one hand, maybe two fingers, the times he'd come back from his meetings and not smelled like he'd drank a gallon of kerosene.

Her Daddy wasn't alone though. There were a lot of people who wanted what he had in the trunk, which was why they spent all their time going from one new city to another. Hours and hours of doing nothing but watching houses, trees and clouds pass by through the back window to fill her days. Sometimes, her father would come out of a store with a newspaper or a magazine for her and she was grateful for it. Even though she knew it wasn't because he cared if she was bored. He didn't. He wasn't doing anything nice for her. He knew reading would keep her quiet and that was truly all he cared about. She wasn't imagining his coldness. It was very much real, and she felt it every minute of every day.

"Here! Take these and read. Read and read *quietly!*" he'd yell at her as he tossed whatever magazine or newspaper he'd grabbed to keep her quiet. He absolutely hated it when she tried to talk to him.

"Jesus H. Christ, August, can't you do anything except run your trap all the time?"

She didn't understand how he thought she could go for days without uttering a single word to him, but it's exactly what he expected of her. All he wanted to do was drive his car to the next "sale" and forget that she was even alive in the seat behind him.

August had about finished filling the tank when her father came around the corner of the gas station, tucking his shirt into the waist of his trousers. The station clerk straightening her dress and fussing over her hair, was right behind him.

His face turned beet red when he noticed the trunk lid open. He stormed over to her and furiously slammed the lid shut so hard that August jumped back. Grabbing her by both arms, he started shaking her as sweat poured from his forehead.

"How many goddamned times did I tell you to NEVER, EVER get into my business?"

He shook her so hard she was beginning to see tiny little dots falling in front of her eyes. August began to feel like something in her head was shaking loose. She tried to speak to him.

"Daddy, I didn't mean…"

"Didn't mean to? Oh, don't give me that cock and bull story! Nobody does nothing they don't *mean* to do. I told you, didn't I? I told you exactly what was going to happen if you didn't mind your p's and q's. But you just couldn't listen could ya?! Now you're going to be sorry, girl! *Very* Sorry."

Not once in her whole life had August seen that kind of anger and rage in his eyes. She'd seen him drunk plenty of times and he'd get mad if she weren't quiet while he wanted to sleep. But this was a kind of angry she'd never seen before. Ever.

He pushed August away hard. At which point,

she lost her footing and fell to the ground beside the pump. He lit a cigarette and ran his hand through his slicked back head of greasy hair. He blew puffs of white smoke into the air frantically. He was thinking hard and that scared her. He liked things to go the way he wanted them to go and if they didn't, he had to think of a solution and he didn't like to have to do that. He'd told her that many times too.

"Thinking too hard causes a head to hurt, hair to turn gray and ages a man too damned quick" he'd told her more times than she could count.

Looking at the jars in the trunk, made him mad all over again. He stomped his foot and kicked a pop top out of the way with enough force to send it clear across the parking lot.

If she could be quiet now and not let him hear so much as a rustle of her pillow in the backseat, maybe he'd forget all those threats that sounded more like promises, about the orphanage thing. She crossed her fingers and squeezed her eyes closed, real tight and made a wish to the wide-open sky and any stars that might be hiding behind the rain clouds. *"Please let Daddy forgive me for nosing around and let me sit back here still as still can be and maybe will forget all about it."* she wished silently.

She'd made that wish on every star she figured existed in the universe before finally falling asleep. Hours later, she was awakened by the slamming of the driver's door. August could tell by the tone in her Daddy's voice that he'd been drinking again. Not that it was unusual for him to be drunk..

"Hey! Kid! You awake back there?"

Her heart raced. She didn't know what to do. Make him mad by not answering him or make him mad by speaking? When he yelled louder a second time, she figured she'd better answer. She did her best to lightly respond like she would have if she really had been asleep.

"Yes, Daddy?"

"Yeah! That's what I figured. I knew you were awake and faking sleep. Sneaky little thing you've become haven't you?"

"I'm not being sneaky, Daddy. I just..." He interrupted and cut her off. Dismissing whatever it was she had to say with the wave of his hand.

"Don't even bother! You weren't pretending to be asleep just like you *accidently* popped open the trunk. I know. I know. Innocent little August."

"But really, Daddy, honest to God, I really didn't mean to..."

"Oh yes, I know. That trunk just popped itself right open all on its own."

He laughed aloud in a sinister tone that August didn't like. It was an evil laugh that scared her half to death. There was something very menacing in the tone that she hadn't heard before. Cold chills popped up all over her body. Until that moment, she'd never *really* been afraid of him. He pulled down the rearview mirror until he could see her clearly and his eyes seemed to look right through her.

"Don't you worry yourself about one little thing, girl. Everything's going to be all right. For *me* anyway." That laugh again. This time August felt her body start to tremble.

He went on, "Got me a deal with one of my acquaintances. Yep. We done made ourselves a deal that solves *all* my problems and washes my troubles right down the drain. I ain't going to have to worry about you sticking your nose where it doesn't belong no more. Not come tomorrow anyway."

What was he talking about? What deal? What acquaintance and what did any of that have to do with her?

He slapped the steering wheel and started laughing out loud again. She didn't know what he was talking about but could tell by the evil cackling that it was not something she was not going to like. Not one bit. August dug deep inside for strength to steady her voice as she asked, "A deal Daddy? I don't know what you mean by that."

All the sudden, he grabbed the steering wheel with one hand and the back of the seat with the other. When he'd turned completely around to face her, she could clearly see the scariest look she'd ever seen on anyone's face. It was the kind of smile that told every nerve in her body to open the car door and run away as fast as she could. She should have listened to her gut. Had she known what he had in store for her, she would have. Lord knows she should have.

CHAPTER TWO

The next morning, her father drove to the nearest gas station and yelled at August to wake up as he threw open the back door of the car.

"Get out and go clean yourself up. Put on some clean clothes and brush those rats nests out of your hair while you're at it." he ordered.

August did as she was told. She locked the restroom door behind her and stared at her face in the mirror. Something didn't feel good in the pit of her stomach. Since when did her father care about whether she was clean or if she brushed her hair? Why now? What was going on inside his head behind those crazy eyes she'd seen the night before?

As she washed up in the greasy sink, she could feel

that something in her world was about to change. A shift was coming, and panic swept through every bone in her body. She realized there wasn't anything she could do to stop whatever her father was up to. She hadn't had time to finish brushing out the knots in her hair when she jumped at the pounding on the door.

"You about done in there or what? I got places to go and people to see. I didn't tell you to take all day did I?"

"I'm almost done, Daddy. I'll be out soon."

"You better be. If you're not, then I'm coming in to get ya. You can count on it." he threatened.

She could tell by the sound of his voice that she'd somehow managed to irritate him again without meaning to. She hurried to brush through her ratty hair and threw on a cotton dress that was "mostly" clean. It was the best dress she owned, which wasn't saying much. All her clothes were too small and had become worn so thin that daylight could be seen through the fabric.

Her father's clothes, now that was a different story. He washed his often and paid people to iron them and always looked like an important businessman in his fancy suits. It was all part of how he managed to put food in her mouth, he'd told her. Since she hardly ever saw other people, it wasn't important what she wore or how often she bathed. That was his opinion, but August was getting old enough to see that having a bath and wearing clean clothes would be nice. She wished she had an opportunity to have both more often, but she didn't. As her father said, "if wishes were horses, we'd all have a ride."

At one point, she tried hand washing a dress and her underclothes in a gas station sink and hung them in the back window of the car to dry. Her father snatched them down in a hurry saying it looked "trashy." The man drove around the country with his child in the back of the car while he sold illegal liquor to criminals, yet he worried about *her* making him look trashy.

How she kept herself or what she wore was never a concern for him before. Until now. Why was he suddenly so concerned about those things? Something was wrong but she couldn't figure it out yet.

The pounding on the door started again just as she was about to reach for the doorknob. He pushed open the door at the same time. "I told you I was coming in for you if you didn't make it snappy, didn't I?"

"I hurried as fast as I could, Daddy."

"Well as usual, it wasn't fast enough! Now get out of here and back into the car. We have people to meet."

August wanted to know where they were going and who they were meeting. She didn't meet people, *that* was his job, not hers. Not once in her entire life had he brought her to meet someone. She had *never* met his "friends" or acquaintances. Butterflies (the bad kind) whizzed throughout her body, just under her skin. She'd always wished she could meet one of the people her father went to "visit" with but now that the time was here, she was not feeling excited about it at all. Something was off with her father and the entire situation. She didn't know exactly what it was, but she knew it didn't feel good. Not even a tiny little bit.

They drove to yet another back alley that looked like every other alley they'd spent so much time in. They all looked alike. Dark with trash thrown everywhere even though there were trash cans lined up behind the back doors of the businesses, it appeared they were not used regularly. Most of the time there was a drunken bum or two leaning against the wall or on the ground talking to himself. Dark alleys gave her the willies ever since that time in New Orleans.

She'd been in the car waiting for her father to come back from his "meeting." She was lying in the back seat reading a comic book that her father had given her the week before. Her face was buried in it, even though she'd read it at least twenty times already. She hadn't noticed the drunken wino who had shuffled up to the car until he opened the back door. She remembered the incoherent mumbling and the awful smell of alcohol mixed with rotten old trash. The drooling man tried to get into the car with her.

August was kicking at him and screaming as he tried to shush her. "Stop that now, girl! All I wants a dollar. You got a dollar I can have?"

She kept kicking and screaming until he backed himself out of the car. She slammed the door shut and locked both sides of the car up tight. Every time her father left the car after that, she locked the doors as soon as he was out of sight.

She'd told her father about that incident at the time,

and she thought he'd be upset that such a thing had happened to his little girl. She should have known better. It was *her* fault for keeping her nose buried in her book and not paying attention. She was six years old at the time. She didn't know much about parenting but as she grew older and thought back on that incident, she realized that kids don't know anything when they are young unless a parent teaches them. Her father did and continued to have, other ideas about all of that. She realized later that her father had a lot of ideas about things that weren't necessarily clever ones.

Such as the back alley they had just pulled into. She was about to leave the haven of safety in the back seat and go out into a dark, nasty smelling alley, which went against everything she had known up until that point. If it weren't the first time she'd ever gone to meet someone with her father, she may not have been afraid. But it *was* the first time.

She tried to get up the courage to ask him more about why she was going to meet his "friends." But every time she'd thought about speaking up, she saw a scowl on his face in the rearview mirror. It was the closed off look he had that said "Don't talk to me. Don't bother me. Do what you are told."

He opened the back door and motioned for her to get out. Looking her over, he told her to twirl around so he could see if she looked "good enough." When she had turned to face him again, he was spitting into his handkerchief scowling. He threw it at her and told her to wash her face.

"Damn it, girl! I told you to wash your face in the restroom back at the station. Can't you EVER do what you're told? Just once?"

August took the handkerchief, damp with her father's spit, which wreaked of moonshine and rolled it over her cheeks. She *had* washed her face earlier but telling him that would have just angered him more than he already was. He was always angry. She couldn't remember a time when he wasn't. It was who he was. It was just his way she figured. He was upset and mad at something every day. It came as natural to him as breathing.

When he conceded that she'd done a good enough job, he yanked the handkerchief from her and stuffed it back into his jacket pocket. He reached for her hand, and she instinctively jumped back a bit. His big sweaty hand gripped her little hand even harder.

"What the hell do you think you're doing?" he yelled.

She wanted to say that he was hurting her hand, but instead she said nothing and let the tears burn at her eyelids.

"Oh, knock off the crybaby bit. That's the last thing I need to deal with today. You hear me?"

She wiped her eyes and nodded in agreement. Mr. Finnegan yanked her arm and dragged her forward against her will. She tripped over her own feet, but he didn't stop. She didn't know why but her body wasn't cooperating with her at all. It was as if it knew she should not be going where she was going and was trying to stop her from making a big mistake.

They continued down the alley before coming to a large red door. It looked just like all the others in the alley, except that it was painted a very *bright* red.

Her father knocked on the door in a strange pattern of knocks. Three short knocks followed by a pause. Then five more knocks in a row. August felt her body flinch when a small door about eye level to her father slid open quickly. She couldn't see who was behind the door but a stern, gruff voice asked, "Going to rain today?" August thought it was an odd thing for him to say.

Even odder was her father's response of "be a good day in Spain if it don't rain."

She was totally confused now. Neither of them made any sense. Whatever they were talking about must have made sense to them because the window slid shut and she heard the sound of locks sliding on the other side of the door. Slowly, the large, heavy door opened, and her father yanked her inside. She was surprised to see an incredibly small man standing there in front of her. He was even smaller than she was. He jumped down from the stool he'd been standing on behind the door and she realized he came up to about her waist, but he wasn't a child. He was an older man who just hadn't grown tall like most men.

"You here for Big John?"

"Not today. Today I've come to see Sal."

The little man raised an eyebrow. "That so? He knows you're coming?"

"He does. Should be expecting me about now." her father replied.

The man yelled into a dark hallway to his left. "Junior! Tell Sal he's got company. Make sure he knows it's a man with a kid who's here to see him."

A taller, skinny man that looked like he'd never seen a drop of sunlight in his whole life stepped out from the darkness. His face was as white as a sheet and his hair about the same color. August had never seen anyone like him before. She thought to herself that he looked like more of a ghost than a live human being.

The little man sat down on his stool as they waited. "So, what business ya got bringing a kid around here, Mister?"

August was surprised to hear her father snap at the man in the same tone he always used with her. Is that how he talked to everyone? "I'd prefer you mind your own beeswax. My business is with Sal and you ain't Sal."

The little man scowled. "Geeze, Mister. Calm down. I was just being friendly is all."

"Didn't come to make friends. Came to see Sal. Appreciate it if you don't bother me with idle chit chat and nonsense while I wait."

"Sure. Sure. No problem. What about you, young lady? How are you today? he asked.

Her father squeezed her hand again. Hard. Too hard. "Appreciate it if you don't talk to her neither."

"Oh. I see. Okay. Sure, Mister. Have it your way." He looked down at the nails on his stubby, little fingers and started fidgeting with a hangnail.

The other man finally returned and told August and her father to follow him. Another door opened and she could hear it lock behind them. *What kind of place was this?* They stood inside a small barely lit room with yet another closed door in front of them.

Her father let go of her hand for a minute and she was glad for it.

The tall man rapped a series of knocks on the door just as her father had done back in the alley. Another window slid open, and another man's voice answered through the little window.

"Yes?"

"Got company for Sal."

Whoever was on the other side of the door didn't say a word just slammed the window shut with a thud. The door opened and August could hear music playing. As her father dragged her inside, he knelt to speak to her at eye level.

"Now listen to me, girl. And listen well. Do you hear me? This is important."

"Yes, Daddy. I hear you."

"Good. Now you stay with me, and you do *exactly* what I say. There won't be any questions out of you and that's just the way it's going to be. This is the end of you not listening to me!"

August didn't like the sour taste that was rising from her stomach and sitting at the back of her throat, but she nodded in agreement. What else could she do?

Looking around the room there was a large crowd of people. All of them dressed in fancy clothes. The women wore beautifully colored dresses, and the men wore black suits with colored handkerchiefs in the breast pocket of their jackets. August thought they looked like the movie stars she had seen in the newspaper. A couple of the men even wore black top hats. Most were sitting at tables playing cards or eating dinner. Some were standing around a table with a spinning wheel bouncing a little ball around, as they yelled, "Come on black or come on red!"

Her father dragged her through the room quickly but not quick enough. Two men started to whistle and yell, "Hey! Mister, where'd you find that little cutie? She got a sister?" They laughed loudly but her father wasn't laughing, he kept a tight grip on her hand as he led her through the room.

They headed toward a mostly hidden door behind a bar that had more drinking glasses lined up than she'd ever seen before. The man knocked on the wall and a door opened.

"Company for Sal." he said, and the door opened all the way. He didn't go inside but motioned for them to go on in."

August's hand was almost numb now from her father squeezing it so tight. After the door closed behind them, he let go of her hand like it was on fire and distanced himself a few feet away from her.

CHAPTER THREE

As her eyes adjusted to the darkness of the room, August was in awe of the red painted walls. She'd never seen a room painted in red with gold trim borders. It was most certainly the fanciest place she'd ever been! Surprisingly, the room was dark even with the bright red walls. The lack of windows was apparent as her eyes adjusted to the darkness.

Behind a large black desk, also with gold trim adorning the edges, sat a large bald man. He didn't appear to be tall in stature but round in size. He looked like he was very warm as he was sweating profusely and had to keep wiping his brow with a cloth. Streams of water pooled on his forehead and ran down the sides of his chubby, round face. A face that looked scary to August and not the least bit friendly.

When he'd wiped his brow for about the tenth time since they'd been inside, he yelled to someone outside the door. His voice was very loud and demanding. August doubted anyone would dare disobey him. She could feel that he wielded that kind of power. She decided right away that she didn't like him. She looked over at her father, who also seemed oddly nervous. He kept shifting his weight from one foot to the other, in a way that she hadn't seen him do before.

"Jerry, bring me a cool cloth and a handful of clean handkerchiefs, and I don't intend to be waiting half the day for them! Understood?" he bellowed, and August jumped at the deep roar of his voice.

When Jerry shut the office door, the fat man settled his gaze on August. Turning away now and again to stare at her father. He looked at them as though he hadn't known they'd been standing in front of him all the while. He didn't say a word at first, just squinted his eyes from time to time and surveyed them like he was oblivious as to why they were there.

Her father spoke first. "Sal, this here's…"

Sal bellowed and interrupted. "I didn't ask you to address me did I?"

Her father shook his head and Sal continued, "When I want you to open your trap, I'll let you know. Until then, shut it."

"Yes sir" her father answered cowardly as he talked into his shoes.

Suddenly the ruler of her entire world had shrunk into a small little man. He seemed to have lost every bit of backbone he had possessed when he'd come through the door. It felt strange and totally out of character to see him afraid. She'd always seen him as a man in control. A man who let her know regularly that HE was in charge.

Sal continued looking them over. He scowled every now and again but didn't say a word. Finally, he pointed at August and spoke. His tone a little softer than he had used with her father, but there was still a sternness to it that said he wasn't going to take any back talk from anyone.

"Turn around girl!"

She stepped closer to her father and grabbed his hand. She looked up at him unsure of what she was supposed to do. He yanked his hand away from her like he'd done earlier, as though she'd had the plague or something infectious.

"Don't look at me. Do what you're told." he demanded.

She looked back at Sal who was rotating his finger as he repeated for her to twirl herself around.

"I ain't got all day for this nonsense. She does what I say or we ain't got us a deal. Ya got it?"

"Yes Sir." her father stated firmly.

He grabbed August by the arm and pulled her closer to the desk. "You heard the man, now do it!"

She looked at him and then at Sal. She wanted so badly to ask why she was supposed to spin around in front of this strange man, but she knew better. The tone of her father's voice was deeper and meaner than she'd ever heard him use before. She knew this was not a time to cross him.

She slowly turned back toward the door she'd come through and back around until she was once again facing the desk.

Sal scrunched up his face. "Ain't much to work with there that I can see."

"She can do whatever you want her to do Sal. I tell ya she can and she's a real fast learner too."

Sal raised his eyebrows and grumbled. "So *you* say."

John Finnegan spoke in a pleading, almost begging manner. "Really, Sal, she *can* do things and if ya got somebody to teach her, she can learn about anything. I know she ain't much of a looker now, but if she fixed herself up… if someone showed her how, she could be the looker that her Ma was. She ain't got nobody but me and I don't know nothing about the womanly kind of things a girl ought to know. Rum running, I know. Woman things, not so much."

Sal picked up a pen and was tapping it on the desk the entire time her father was speaking. Just then, Jerry brought in a stack of handkerchiefs and a wet cloth on a silver tray.

Sal grabbed the tray away from Jerry's hands. "I said I wasn't going to wait all day, didn't I Jerry? You didn't hear me say that?"

Jerry looked at the floor. "Yes, sir. I heard it and I came as fast as I could."

He spat on the floor at Jerry's feet. "That was anything BUT fast. When I tell you I want something, I want it then, not when you feel like it. How many times I got to tell you this, Jer?"

Without warning, Sal reached over and hit Jerry hard with a fist to his stomach. She heard a tiny noise escape from Jerry's mouth as he gasped for air. He slowly stood himself up from the bent over position he'd taken after the punch to his gut.

"Yes, sir." He answered. "Next time I'll do better, Boss."

Sal stared straight into August's eyes as he spoke to Jerry. "Good man, Jerry. You know I'm not a man to tolerate people not listening to me. Now let us be."

Jerry walked out of the room as fast as his long stick-like legs would carry him. Still, Sal never took his eyes from August. "Now, where were you and I, young lady?"

Neither she nor her father made a peep. Looking up at him, she decided he didn't feel much like her father at all at that moment. He should have been defending her against this strange, mean man who was giving her the creeps. But he wasn't. He had quickly turned into a stranger and one she didn't trust.

"So, what do you say, Sal? We got a deal?"

August was trying to decipher what they were talking about. A deal? A deal for what? As hard as she tried, she couldn't make the connection in her mind. What did selling this man moonshine have to do with her twirling around in front of him?

Sal laughed out loud. "Like I said, you ain't got nothing too special there that I can see. Still, if we got that ratty old dress off her and a good scrubbing, eh, who knows, she might be worth it."

August realized they were talking about her, and

her eyes grew wider. What was going on here? They were talking about getting *her* dress off? She didn't care who this Sal person was or how everyone was afraid of him, including her father. *No one* was getting her dress off or going to be giving her any kind of scrubbing and she had every intention of making sure of it.

She put her hands on her hips and said, "No." It was more of a whisper, but she'd said it just the same. Neither of them heard her but she'd worked up the nerve to defend herself. When August realized that neither of them was paying attention to her, she said it again, but louder. "No!"

Sal's laughter practically shook the room. "*No?*" he grabbed his chest and laughed even louder.

August stood her ground and wasn't about to back down. If her father were too much of a coward to stand up to this man on her behalf, she'd do it herself.

"No!" she repeated.

Her father grabbed her arm and told her to be quiet.

Sal stopped him, "No, no, don't stop her. She's a little spitfire like I haven't seen in a long, long time. Let her go. I find her quite amusing." he said in between bouts of laughter.

August could feel her face getting warmer and her heart raced more by the second. Neither Sal nor her father was taking her seriously, but she didn't care.

Sal stopped laughing and his face turned serious. He opened a drawer of his desk and pulled out a fat, brown envelope. He opened it and stared at its contents carefully.

"Alright. You got yourself a deal. Two hundred just liked we talked about. Here you go. The deal is, you leave here today and don't ever think about coming back, you hear me? A deal's a deal."

Her father slowly walked toward the desk and took the envelope from him. "Yes sir. A deal is a deal."

He walked right past August like he didn't even know her. His eyes low and not looking in her direction in the least bit. She followed him to leave.

"No. You ain't coming with me this time. You do what you're told, you hear me?" he demanded.

August grabbed his hand and cried, "No Daddy, you can't mean that. Please don't leave me here! I'll be good, I promise I will."

All at once August understood. This was the punishment for looking in the trunk when he had warned her not to. Her father had threatened to bring her to the orphanage for years, but that wasn't what he was doing at all. He was leaving her there with Sal. She didn't want to believe that he could or would really do that to her. If this was his way of scaring her to behave, then it was working because she was downright terrified. Her father looked down at her with the iciest look she had ever seen in his eyes. He seemed like someone she didn't even know.

"Oh, I know you'll be good. You're not going to have a choice about that anymore. But you'll be good, right here. This is the end of the line for you and me, kid. I tried to keep my promise, I really did. And I kept it for as long as I could. I just ain't got no more patience left."

August didn't even try to wipe the tears that were streaming down her face. There was no point in trying to stop them from falling because there were a million more right behind them.

"I'm sorry, Daddy for whatever I did. If this is because I saw what was in the back of the car, I'm sorry. I promise I won't tell a soul what I saw. I promise I won't. From now on, you won't hear a single sound from me. Just take me with you. Please Daddy, don't leave me here." she begged him.

She dug her little hands deeper into the hem of his shirt. She wasn't letting go. She could not stay there with these people.

Sal put his feet up on the desk. "Deals a deal, kid. Jerry, come in here this instant!"

Jerry ran into the room. "Yes sir?"

"Grab that kid off her old man so he can leave, will ya?"

Jerry was a skinny man, but he was strong. In one quick motion, he grabbed onto her back and pulled her free from her father. August thrashed her legs and arms and screamed for him to let her down, but Jerry dangled her from his long arms and her feet were unable to touch the floor.

"Daddy, help me! Please, Daddy!" she cried.

Over the child's screams, Sal roared, "Take her to Rosa, Jerry. She'll know what needs to be done. As for you, Mister, it's like I said. Don't ever think about coming back here again or you'll be sorry you did. There's the door, I suggest you go through it."

Without so much as a glance back at his daughter,

John Finnegan opened the door and walked through it as though he hadn't just left his only child behind with complete strangers. As if he hadn't just sold his child to a total stranger for two hundred dollars. That's what her life was worth to him. Two hundred measly dollars.

CHAPTER FOUR

Jerry carried her over his shoulder, oblivious to her kicking and thrashing the entire way to the basement. Where was he taking her? And who was this Rosa woman she was going to see? August was getting the feeling that she was about to be locked in a dark basement for the rest of her life. Not that there was a single living soul who would care if she was. There was no one coming to her rescue. The one person who was supposed to care for her, had just sold her for pocket money, as though she were a crate of moonshine whiskey. How was selling your own child not an illegal activity worse than selling illegal liquor? Surely it had to be a crime. Illegal or not, it had happened. She had witnessed the deal with her own eyes. For as long as she lived, she'd never forget the heartless look on her father's face as he left her behind. And for what reason? Because she'd seen a load of moonshine liquor in his trunk when it was supposed to be some big secret?

What did she care if he was running illegal booze? It wasn't like she was the coppers or that she'd ever tell anyone. Who was there to tell anyway? She wouldn't know the first thing about turning him in. The only reason she knew it was illegal to begin with was because she'd read about prohibition in a newspaper. That first time she'd ever read a newspaper was burned into her memory as a momentous day. She'd been trying to have a conversation with her father, who as usual, didn't want to indulge her in idle chat. He tossed a newspaper at her and told her to see what was going on in the world and leave him be.

They had parked in an endless sea of cornstalks in a field somewhere outside a town called Moline so her father could rest for a bit. She'd taken the newspaper with her and left the car to find a spot to read while her father napped. The cornfield was so big it was like a giant maze. For as far as her eyes could see, there had been nothing but corn. She'd dragged her worn old blanket from the car and made her own little cabin amongst the stalks. Her very own space that she didn't have to share. She remembered how independent she felt to have a tiny space, even if temporary, of her own. It was there in that little cabin she'd made for herself that she learned about prohibition and of the depression. Neither were something that her father had ever mentioned to her. But on that day, in that cornfield, she'd felt like she had come as close to heaven as she'd ever be. Nothing around but the sound of the wind rushing through the corn and the sound of birds chirping somewhere in the distance. It was all hers for a time. Until her father woke up and yelled for her to get back in the car. All of that seemed like ages ago now.

None of that mattered anymore. The fact was her father had taken money in exchange for his daughter. Something she would never, ever forgive or forget. He'd left her with complete strangers who had no good intentions. She could feel that in her gut. The henchman who currently had her thrown over his shoulder, dragging her down into a dark basement, against her will, did not give the impression that these were kind, sweet people. What hurt so much more though, was that her father hadn't kept his promise to her mother. He could tell himself that he had kept it all he wanted, but in her mind, he'd ripped that promise up and thrown it into thin air like an overdue letter from the bank.

"Where are you taking me? Where am I? Let me go!" she continued to scream. But it didn't matter, the man just kept walking.

Finally, he stopped and opened a door at the end of the hall. She could smell fresh bread as soon as he cracked open the door. The sound of clanging pots and pans echoed loudly through her head.

"Ms. Rosa, what are you cooking today? Sure does smell delicious whatever it is." he commented.

She couldn't see Rosa from where he stood but heard the raspy voice of an older woman.

"Oh, don't be trying to butter me up you big oaf. What the hell are you doing in my kitchen and why on earth do you have a child flung over your shoulder?"

"Huh?" he asked as though he had completely forgotten that there was a human being slung over his shoulder. "Oh, her. Sal says to bring her to you."

"To me? What the hell for?"

Jerry shrugged his shoulders.

"You don't know? Well, that makes two of us you idiot. Now, put that poor kid down!" she demanded.

August felt dizzy when he finally set her down and her feet could touch the floor again. Her knees were like jelly about to buckle under her. She grabbed onto a stool next to the table to steady herself.

The old woman walked over to her and stood beside her. She reached for August's shoulder and the girl instinctively jumped back. She'd had enough of being pushed aside and carried against her will. One more person pawing over her was just not going to happen.

"Oh my! Jumpy lil thing aren't you?" she asked.

August squinted her eyes and practiced her best scowl. "Just don't touch me. I don't want to be touched. Not by you. Not by HIM and certainly not by that creepy Sal. All of you just leave me alone!" she yelled at the absolute top of her lungs.

Rosa backed up a step. "Alright child, alright. Calm yourself down. No one's going to touch you. Please sit. You look like you could use some food."

August didn't want to admit that she was starving

but she was. She'd eaten peanuts from a store the day before with a soda pop to wash it down. That was the meal her father had given her that day. She wanted to be able to refuse whatever food this woman planned on putting in front of her. She wanted to be able to shove it away and not touch a single bite. She wanted to, but she knew she was hungry enough to eat whatever the woman was about to offer.

"What's your name, child?" she asked.

Jerry, who was still in the room spoke before August could answer. "Rosa, what you got around here for a sandwich?"

Rosa whacked a dish towel against the table. "Can't you see that I'm trying to talk to this young lady, you big lug? WHAT are you still doing in my kitchen? You know the rules you heathen! I don't care what you want to eat! You stay the hell out of my kitchen, and you wait until dinner is served UPSTAIRS." she reminded him.

Jerry looked at the floor. "Yes Ma'am."

August wanted to smile or laugh out loud, but she didn't. The last thing she needed was Rosa turning the tirade in her direction. Still, she thought it quite humorous that the giant slug of a man had been told what's what by a woman half his size.

After he'd left the kitchen, Rosa sat across the table from her. She had two bowls sitting on the table. Slowly, she slid one toward August, who crossed her arms in front of her and looked away.

"I'm going to have myself some dinner. There's plenty here since I cook for the customers upstairs.

Would you like to join me?"

August continued to look away up into the corner of the room. "So be it, child. So be it. I've been working my fingers to the bone, and I need a bite to eat. If you don't then you don't. Either is ok by me."

She carried a pot of something from the wood cook stove at the opposite side of the room. August tried to eye what she had in the pot without being too obvious. When Rosa poured a ladle of beef stew into the bowl in front of herself, August swore the delicious smell wafting in the air had come straight from heaven. Steaming hot stew with potatoes and carrots in a beef broth was something she hadn't had in what seemed like forever. The last time had been maybe a year earlier at a diner they'd stopped at in the middle of the night.

To make matters worse, Rosa came back with an entire loaf of fresh baked white bread and set it on the table. As she began to cut the bread, August could hold out no more.

"I'd like some of that please." She barely whispered but Rosa heard her fine.

"Was hoping you might. Nothing worse than eating a delicious meal all by your lonesome. Food always tastes so much better when it's shared with someone."

August heard her stomach growl loudly in anticipation as her bowl was being filled. Rosa buttered two slices of bread and set them next to her bowl. The first spoonful made August feel like she could cry. It was the best thing she'd ever tasted in her entire life. The second bowl was even better.

She couldn't get the food onto her spoon and into her mouth fast enough. A lifetime of quick foods or snacks did not compare in any way to the homecooked meal she was being treated to. Rosa seemed pleased that her cooking was being thoroughly enjoyed.

"Slow down child. There's plenty more where that came from. You don't want to choke on your dinner."

She slid two more slices of buttered bread across the table. "May I have another bowl?"

Rosa laughed. "Of course you can. Been a while since you've eaten a homecooked meal or just any ole meal in general?" she asked.

August wanted to tell her that she'd never in her entire life eaten a meal that tasted that good. But she didn't. She didn't know her. She didn't want to know her and had no intentions of staying long enough to get to know her. Or Jerry. Most certainly, not Sal. As soon as she could make a run for it, she was going to do just that. She didn't even care where she went, she just knew she wasn't staying there. Wherever "there" was.

For the time being, she'd eat until she was full. This Rosa woman didn't seem to be all that bad. At least she didn't creep her out like Jerry and Sal. Plus, she was giving her a delicious meal. August decided that Rosa could be tolerated for as long as she needed to deal with her.

When she couldn't eat one more bite, August pushed the bowl away and leaned back in the wooden chair. Her eyes felt heavy. Now that she had eaten, she felt like she could sleep for days. Rosa must have noticed her yawning because she said, "Nothing like a satisfying meal and a nap, I say. What about you, child? You tired?"

August hated to admit that she was, but she was exhausted.

"Alright then, Ms.?" She paused for August to tell her what she should call her. After thinking about it for a minute, she realized it would do no harm to let Rosa know what her name was. She had shown her kindness, which was more than she could say for the big jerk that had thrown her over his shoulder and trudged down the stairs with her. And she certainly wasn't as nasty as sweaty Sal.

"August. My name is August."

Rosa smiled. "Mine's Rosa, but I guess you already know that. It's nice to meet you, Ms. August. I'm sure you have a million questions about what's going on here and to be honest, so do I. But for the time being, let's get you some rest and we'll worry about the rest bum-bye. That sound okay to you?"

August nodded in agreement as she yawned out loud, though she hadn't meant to. Rosa motioned for her to follow her as she pulled back a curtain at the far end of the kitchen. Inside was a cot, neatly made among the shelves of preserved fruits and vegetables.

"This here is where I stay some nights when it's too late for me to walk home. Today, it's yours young lady. You sure do look like you need this old cot a whole lot more than I do right now."

August laid down and Rosa covered her with an old quilt.

"I'm afraid it's not going to be exactly quiet down here. Pots and pans clanging and such due to it being dinner time and all. Lots of customers upstairs to feed. Somehow, I don't think anything will be bothering you too much though. Sleep well, child."

She was right. As soon as August heard her pull the curtain closed, she drifted off into a warm, dark sleep.

CHAPTER FIVE

Loud voices woke August out of a sound sleep. "I said you are to leave her be, and that's damned well what's going to happen. Now get out of my kitchen, and I won't be telling you again!" demanded Rosa.

August quickly got up and peeked around the curtain that separated the make-shift bedroom from the kitchen. There was Rosa, a tiny woman, not five feet tall with a stout, sturdy roundness to her, laying down the law to the big ape of a man, Jerry. Though she was small in height, August could see that Rosa was a force to be reckoned with. After she'd seen her kick Jerry out of her kitchen the night before, it was obvious that little Rosa wasn't afraid of anyone. Certainly not Jerry.

"But Ms. Rosa, Sal told me to get…"

Rosa's voice was louder this time. "And I told you NO! You can tell Sal if he wants her, he'll have to come down here and deal with me himself."

"Oh, c'mon Rosa. You know I can't do that."

Rosa laughed. "No. I suppose you can't. Seeing how every inch of your backbone was removed the day you met Sal."

Silence filled the room. "Well, what are you waiting for? You heard what I said. The child is resting and she's going to continue resting. Nothing more to talk about. Now say goodbye and get out of my kitchen!"

August heard Jerry's footsteps and the slam of the kitchen door, followed by Rosa's sighs of victory. "Ha! Big ole dummy thinks he can come into MY kitchen and throw his weight around. He's got another thing coming."

Rosa was stirring something in a large bowl as she grumbled to herself. Her hands turning the spoon around faster and faster as she went. August could see that her face was flushed as she mumbled to herself. Although her voice was lower now, August could still hear an occasional, "I'll show him" or "Don't come in here telling *me* what I need to do."

At that moment, she knew she would be safe with Rosa. She didn't know August or anything about her and she didn't have to protect her from Jerry, but she had. Twice now. Maybe her mother in heaven had seen what a monster John Finnegan had turned out to be and had sent her this kind woman to look after her. Even if it weren't true, it was what August decided she would believe from that moment on.

She stepped into the kitchen where Rosa spotted her out of the corner of her eye. "Well good morning, sleepyhead." she said with a smile on her face.

She sat a bowl on the table and walked toward August. She reached her arms out to rest her hands on the young girl's shoulders and this time, August did not pull away.

"Rest well did you, child?

"I did."

"That's good. Sometimes life just kicks us in the backside and sucks all the life out of a body. A hot meal and good night's sleep is a recipe for a brand-new day that always looks a lil brighter. At least that's what I tell myself."

She smiled and this time, August smiled back at her. Rosa led her to a sink where she could wash up before breakfast. August knew she'd been tired, but she hadn't planned on sleeping so long. It felt like only a minute earlier that she was eating dinner and now it was time for breakfast.

She brushed her hair with her fingers as best she could, which didn't seem to make a lot of difference, but it was better than nothing she supposed. She washed her face and hands and looked down at the crumpled old dress that had seen better days, hanging from a hook on the back of the door.

When she'd finished, Rosa patted the table and pulled out a chair for her. "You just sit right here and take a seat young lady. I'll whip you up a breakfast in no time."

"Thank you, Ms. Rosa, for letting me sleep here. And for feeding me that delicious meal last night. I didn't even know I was that hungry or tired, but I guess I must have been."

"You are most welcome, child. Happy you got yourself rested."

August sat in the chair while Rosa cooked. Neither said a word but both enjoyed the silence. The crackling of the eggs and bacon frying in the pan was the only noise in the room. August tried to remember the last time she'd had fried eggs for breakfast. It had to have been months earlier at a diner somewhere on the road. Come to think of it, it wasn't really breakfast time when they'd stopped at that diner. It was late at night, as it usually was when they were traveling. If her father had a hankering for breakfast at midnight and he could find a place open, that's what he'd have. The time never mattered to August. A hot meal was a hot meal.

"Here you go sweet child. Enjoy." she said as she placed a plate on the table in front of August. "Two eggs, fried potatoes and bacon."

She made a plate for herself and sat down to eat. "So, how is it that you've made your way here to my kitchen in this God forsaken place?"

August took a bite of potatoes and thought about how she should answer the question. What was she supposed to say? Did she admit that her own father sold his flesh and blood to total strangers because he was a no good, drunken moonshine runner? She chewed her food slow as she thought how she should tell Ms. Rosa that she was a throw away child that no one wanted.

"I don't really know." she whispered.

"Well, how about we start at the beginning. Where are your parents?"

August shrugged her shoulders. "I don't know."

"You never knew them?" she asked, setting down her fork.

August took a deep sigh. "Oh, I know my father, I just don't know where he is."

Rosa drank from her coffee mug and looked at her over the rim. "I see. And your mother? Where is she?"

August felt tears begin to sting at the corners of her eyes. She could hear her father's voice in her head. "Don't start that whining business girl! Nobody's got time for that!" She tried hard to stifle the tears she knew were edging closer to falling from beneath her eyelids.

"My mother died when I was a baby, and other than staying with my aunt when I was little, I've been with my father. And yesterday, he'd had enough of keeping a promise to raise me and he left me here. The one person, the *only* person I thought I could trust...left me here with strangers."

"Why here? Did you know Sal before yesterday?"

"No. That's just it Ms. Rosa. I don't know Sal *at all*. I've never been here before and to be honest I don't even know where HERE is."

Rosa sat her coffee cup on the table. "Oh, dear girl. I see you know about as much as I do about the situation. That's okay. Don't you worry about a thing.

Ms. Rosa will get to the bottom of it. I think it's time I go up and have me a talk with Sal."

August felt her heart begin to race. "Would you? Can you ask him where my father went and how I can find him?"

"Hush now. You just sit tight, and I'll be back shortly. In the meantime, get your plate cleaned up. I've left a hairbrush and a bar of soap there at the wash basin for you. You'll find a dress there too. It may be a bit too long, but not as small as what you're wearing."

"I don't know how to thank you for all that you've done for me."

Rosa smiled. "Why, I do believe you just did."

August didn't know where she was, but she knew without question that she was lucky to have met this Rosa woman. She shuddered to think of what may have become of her if the two buffoons upstairs had their way. Fortunately, they'd not had an opportunity. Not yet anyway. Hopefully, they never would. Rosa seemed very intent and determined that no one was going to come into her kitchen and take August. This made her feel safe for the moment, anyway. Maybe things were going to be okay. She was quickly coming to realize that if anyone could get to the bottom of anything, it would be the small, but ever mighty, Ms. Rosa.

CHAPTER SIX

The dress Rosa had laid out on the cot reminded August of something she'd seen older ladies wear. Many times, on Sundays, she and her father had driven past churches and seen people standing around outside socializing. She'd asked her father once what they were all doing there and what *church* was all about. He'd said it was a building that sinners gathered at once a week on Sunday to open their wallets and pay for forgiveness for all the naughty things they'd done during the week. August never understood why people would go to a building with a tall steeple on top, all dressed up in fine clothes, just to open their wallets.

The dress Rosa had given her was cotton like

the others she owned but she couldn't see the light through this one. It had a pattern of small yellow roses with the prettiest white lace all around the collar. She'd never even so much as tried on a dress with lace anywhere on it. She put it over her head and let it fall into place. It was clean, soft, and smelled of fresh air. She inhaled deep and savored the scent. Looking at herself in the mirror, she couldn't help but notice the old denim-blue tennis shoes that were showing from under the dress. She hadn't owned a pair of laces for them since her father took them out, which was almost as soon as he'd bought her the shoes. He'd stripped them from her one day when it had taken her too long to get her feet dressed. She tried as best as she could to tie them like he'd shown her, but she couldn't seem to do it with him yelling at her to do it faster. So, he'd taken them out. Her Aunt tried to teach her a trick about going around the bunny's ears to tie them, but it never stuck in her head. If she didn't run, the sneakers stayed on her feet, so she learned to live without laces.

August took the hairbrush from the sink and ran it through her hair. Her hair was usually tangled when she woke up, and that morning was no exception. Tears pooled in her eyes as she pulled the stiff bristles through the mass of gnarled hair. Her father used to threaten to find a barber to shave it down to her scalp if she didn't learn to take care of it better. The truth was that she'd lost the brush he'd bought her, but she was too afraid to tell him that. She practiced using her fingers to smooth it out well enough so that he hadn't noticed she'd lost the brush. Not that it could have gone far. It was probably buried under the front seat of the car.

Looking at her reflection, she was glad he hadn't ever found that barber. She liked her hair even if it was too long and hard to take care of. She'd been told she had the same jet-black hair and green eyes that her mother had, and somehow that always made her feel connected to a mother she'd never known. It made August happy to know that she looked like the woman who had brought her into this world. She'd never even seen a photo of her though, she was just going on her father's word. Every time she'd not done something fast enough or good enough or if she'd had too many questions, she'd heard the same speech every time. "Can you stop acting just like your mother and do what you're told? Just once? Or just once could you NOT be like your mother and do what you're told?"

The sound of footsteps coming toward the kitchen made her heart begin to race. "Miss August? It's just me, Rosa." she announced.

She stopped dead in her tracks when she came in and saw August. "Well, my goodness, child. Don't you clean up nice!"

August smiled. "Thank you for the dress. It fits so much better than mine."

Rosa smiled. "I see that and it's not too long after all. I'm glad you like it. Now come sit, I'll make us a cup of tea and we can talk."

August did as she was asked even though she didn't know if she liked tea or not. She couldn't remember ever having it. She knew she liked soda pop because that was usually what she'd been given to drink. She had cola for breakfast, lunch, or supper. Still, August was willing to try it because Rosa wanted her too. She hadn't steered her wrong yet.

"Did you talk to Sal? Do you know what's going on?" she asked with anticipation.

"We'll have our tea and I'll tell you what I know. How about a cookie with your tea? I made Snickerdoodles the other day and tucked a few away for myself. Happy to share with you."

August sat back in the chair and waited to hear what Rosa had found out. She hoped to hear that there was some huge mistake and that her father had changed his mind about selling her. Maybe he would give Sal his money back and come to take his daughter back? She sat back in the chair and waited for the tea and cookies and hopefully the good news she was praying for.

CHAPTER SEVEN

Rosa brought two cups of steaming hot tea and a plate of cookies to the table. After taking a sip from her cup, she let out a long exhale as she fidgeted with the strands of white hair that had fallen loose from the bun on top of her head.

"Well, first things first, Little Miss. Let's talk about *you* for a minute."

August wasn't sure what she wanted to talk about. She did know for certain that there wasn't anything interesting about herself to share. "What do you want to know?" No one had ever asked anything about her before.

"Oh, how about you tell me how it is that you and your father knew about this place here."

"I don't really know anything about it, other than what I told you already. My father brought me here yesterday. It was the first time I'd ever been here."

"August, do you know what prohibition is?"

"I know what I've read in the newspaper or heard on the radio. I know that the government is trying to catch people making and carrying moonshine. People like my father. I read about all kinds of arrests they'd made and how they smashed up barrels of liquor that weren't supposed to be sold. Oh, and I've read plenty about that Elliot Ness man who likes to catch bootleggers. I don't know why they call them that, but I did hear that on the radio. I don't know why the government doesn't want people to make or sell it though."

Rosa chuckled. "Well, I see you know a good deal about it then. That's good. I'm glad to hear you can read too."

"No thanks to my Daddy. That's thanks to his sister. I lived with her until I was five."

"Where do you come from originally? What city or state?" she asked.

August shrugged. "I don't know. Daddy said I was born in a hospital somewhere in a place called Kansas. But that's just what I was told. Of course, I can't remember back that far."

"Of course not, child. Nobody can. Is Kansas where you stayed with your aunt?"

"No. I lived in a nice neighborhood outside of Chicago with my Aunt Maggie. It was a good place to live. There were lots of other kids to play with there.

I wish he had left me there and never came back. Of course, I'd still have ended up with Daddy because he said Aunt Maggie died a couple years back."

Rosa scowled. "So, your father really is the only family you have then."

"Yes Ma'am, and now I don't even have him." A solitary tear ran down her cheek.

Rosa reached across the table and took August's hand. "Now, now, things will work out. They will. You'll see."

August smiled and wanted so badly to believe the words Rosa was saying. It felt good to know this woman was someone she could trust. She always thought she could trust her father too, but in the end, he proved that he didn't deserve her trust or respect. Hopefully, this woman didn't let her down too. So far, she hadn't been anything but kind, protective, and August sure hoped she continue to do just that.

Rosa started the conversation again. "The business that Sal runs upstairs is what's called a speak easy, which is a fancy name for a bar. An illegal bar. A place where people come to drink, gamble, dance, eat and are out of view from the police."

It made sense to August now why they had to go through a maze of locked rooms with peephole windows just to get inside.

"There were a whole lot of people up there when we came here that night. Of course, I couldn't see too much on the way downstairs since that buffoon Jerry had me hanging over his back."

"He's a brainless ape for Sal. No brain of his own.

Does what Sal tells him to do. No questions asked. In return, he gets meals and his liquor for free. Don't you worry yourself none about old Jerry, he doesn't scare me a bit and he knows it!"

"What about Sal?" August asked. "Are you afraid of *him*?"

Rosa slowly and deliberately sipped her tea. "Well, Sal's another story my dear. He's a powerful man with a lot of connections around the city. It's not so much that I'm scared of him, it's just that I need to keep a real healthy amount of respect for his boundaries."

"I don't know what that means but I do know I don't like him. He comes down here and tries to take me and I'll haul off and smack him right in the face!"

Rosa laughed out loud. She tried to explain the importance of nobody knowing about what sort of business went on upstairs. "A speak easy is a secret kind of place. A place that *nobody* can know about. If the cops find out about it, they arrest the owner along with all the paying folks inside."

August squinted her eyes as she often did when she didn't understand something. "But people *do* know. All those people eating and drinking upstairs, they all know about it."

"Yes child. Only certain people can know about it, though. People Sal does business with. People he trusts and people he has dirt on. They all come here and know that they can never say a word about the place to anyone. Or else."

"How does he know he can trust *that* many people to keep a secret?"

Rosa chewed on her bottom lip for a minute before answering. "Well, it's like this. The people that come here know that Sal will make them pay if they ever say a word. When I say "pay" I don't mean with money. I mean with their own spilled blood or the blood of their family members. Everyone in this city is afraid of him and for good reason. Sal's a con man, a shyster. He finds out people's dirty laundry, that's what they call a person's secrets. Once he finds out things that people would rather hide, he lets them know that he knows. If they don't want people to know their secrets, then they better not tell his, or he'll make theirs public too. Does that make sense? It's also called "blackmail." Have you ever heard of that word?"

August had never heard of any of what Rosa was telling her before, but her gut told her it was a terrible thing to do, and something that Sal would be good at.

"Just another reason for me to not like that creep."

Rosa laughed. "Oh, my dear girl, there are plenty of reasons folks don't care for that man. You're in good company."

"But what does any of this have to do with *me*, Rosa? I'm not drinking that stuff! I smelled what was in a jar from my Daddy's trunk and I swear it took my breath away. It smelled like gasoline."

"It sure does. Burns like gasoline too. All the way down."

August couldn't imagine why anyone would purposely drink something that seemed like poison.

Rosa reached for her hand. "You remember that Ms. August for the rest of your life. Remember that nasty smell, that way you won't ever want to drink it. Nothing good *ever* comes from the drinking of that nasty stuff. Ms. Rosa knows that firsthand."

"You do? Don't tell me you drink that nasty fire water?"

Rosa smiled. "Well, yes and no. I tried it once when I was younger and that was the only time. It was awful and I didn't like the way it made me feel afterward. Now, my husband, Earl, he was another story. Didn't matter how nasty it tasted or how bad it burned; he was always wanting more. Next thing I knew, he was running with a bad crowd of people who did nothing but drink. And then, he did some terrible things with those people and got himself locked up in the slammer. More than once. Every time they let the dang fool out, he'd go right back to the moonshine."

"Is that where he is now? In the slammer?" August asked.

Rosa shook her head. "No, I'm afraid not. The fool was drinking one night and didn't know enough to not drive. He drove his old jalopy right off the Calhoun bridge. Was a couple of days later when the cops showed up to tell me they'd found his body drowned in the river.

August's eyes grew wide. "He died? I'm sorry to hear that."

Rosa patted August's arm. "Thank you. Served him right though. I kept telling him the liquor was going to kill him one day, but he wasn't going to listen to me. Well, in the end he got his way. Now he doesn't have anyone nagging at him about it no more."

It seemed to August like Rosa wasn't any too sorry about Earl's dying, but she figured there was a lot more to the story that Rosa hadn't told her. She'd remind herself of the story she'd just heard as she grew older, should she ever think she may want to drink alcohol. Although, she doubted she'd ever have an interest in that.

"I am sorry about your husband Rosa. But I still don't understand how any of that has to do with me being here."

"No, I suppose not. I guess I was going around Robin Hood's barn to get to that. Sometimes things take time to get to. Like slowly ripping a bandage off, if you know what I mean?"

August had no idea what she meant. She had no idea how anything Rosa had said so far had to do with her. There was so much that August didn't understand about the whirlwind of events that had taken place in the past few days. Just how alone she was *had* become starkly clear. It was up to her to look out for herself and that was something she'd never once imagined she would have to do at her age.

"I talked with Sal. Seems your father made a deal to sell you to Sal for a couple hundred dollars."

August nodded. "That much I do know. I saw him give Daddy an envelope. When Daddy left without me, I realized that he had sold me the same way he sold those bottles of moonshine. But that's not really what happened is it? He didn't really *sell* me, did he?"

Rosa nodded her head. "I'm afraid it's exactly what happened, Ms. August."

August felt her throat grow tighter and knew that tears weren't far behind. "But why? Why would Daddy do that? I don't understand, Ms. Rosa. I just don't understand. People don't SELL their children, do they?"

"As a rule, no. No, they do not. But there's plenty of folks having a real tough time during this depression. Folks get hard up and hungry and they are likely to do all sorts of things they wouldn't ordinarily do. Sometimes, a family can't afford to feed their kids and they give them to other people to raise. Sometimes for money in return. Other times, they lend their kids out to work and live on other folk's farms where they can have a meal and a bed for the work they do."

August didn't want to believe such a thing. She didn't want to believe that parents could do that to their own children. But she *knew* it happened because it had happened to her. From what Rosa was saying, it was happening to other kids too.

"I just can't figure out why Sal would pay my Daddy money for me. What does he want me for?"

Rosa took a deep breath. "Well, that's the bitter bit as they say. You saw those people upstairs drinking, playing cards and dancing?"

"Yes."

"Well, Sal also has some young ladies who work for him upstairs. He pays them to serve drinks to his customers and girls that do, well, let's just say they do other things for his customers too."

"And he wants me to work for him? But I'm just a *kid*!"

"I said the same words to him myself. But he has his eye on you to do just that. Nothing I said to him was able to sway him away from his crazy notions. Stubborn fool gets an idea in his head and there's no telling him otherwise."

August tried to hold back the tears but there was no stopping them this time. "Whatever it is he wants me to do, I can't do it, Rosa! I won't! I saw those women up there serving drinks and they were half dressed. The clothes they had on were even less than what people wear to bed to sleep in!"

Rosa stood up and held August by the shoulders, giving her whatever little comfort she could. "Alright now, we'll think of something. Now, wipe your eyes and finish your tea. I've got some time with you before he expects you to start learning the ropes upstairs. That gives me time to figure something out."

August hoped Rosa could figure out how to find her father, but in her heart she knew that wasn't ever going to happen. Just like Sal, when her Daddy made his mind up to something, there was nothing that was going to make him change it. He was probably halfway across the state with no plans to come back for her.

For the rest of the day, she helped Rosa in the kitchen. She learned how to peel potatoes and how to handle a sharp knife properly. Once she got the hang of it, she could whip the peelings off a potato in no time at all. When August finished, she had peeled fifteen pounds of potatoes. She felt proud that she had done a decent job in Rosa's eyes. Her parboiled fingers began to cramp but there was no way she would complain. It felt good to learn how to do something she'd never known how to do before.

She even learned how to use a masher. That was the best part of her day. With every thrust of the masher into the soft potatoes, she felt the anger toward her father and Sal wash away, if only for a minute.

When they finished preparing the food, they sent it all upstairs in a dumbwaiter. August was impressed with such a contraption. She wondered who thought of making a door in the wall with a platform inside to send food all the way upstairs. When the staff upstairs emptied the platform, they'd send it back down to the kitchen for more food.

When the kitchen was clean, she and Rosa sat down for their dinner. They had the same meal they had sent upstairs to the paying customers. Mashed potatoes, biscuits, beef roast, and carrots dripping with fresh butter. August decided Ms. Rosa was the best cook in the entire Universe and told her so.

Over the next few days, she helped cook meals and learned how to clean and sanitize a kitchen properly. It was demanding work, but she liked it. She ate better and slept better than she ever had back in her father's car. As the days passed without any word from Sal about her going upstairs to work, part of her hoped that he'd forgotten that she was in the basement with Rosa. The other part of her knew that he wasn't a man who forgot what he paid good money for. She didn't know how long he would let her stay with Rosa, but she prayed every night that it would be for a very long time.

After a week had passed, August realized her prayer to go unnoticed down in the basement was not going to be answered. Rosa sat her down and said they needed to talk. August felt her stomach fall all the way down to the soles of her feet. The look on Rosa's face told her what she feared the most.

CHAPTER EIGHT

Once again, their talk included a hot cup of tea and cookies. August sensed they were meant to ease the pain for whatever uncomfortable conversation was about to follow. August shuddered to think what might have become of her before now if Rosa hadn't stood up to Jerry and Sal that first night she'd come to her kitchen.

"This is one of those talks I'm not going to like isn't it?" she asked, already knowing the answer.

"You're a smart young lady, Ms. August. I'm afraid it is one of those talks that *neither* of us is going to like."

"I was afraid you'd say that."

"This morning while you were asleep, Sal sent for me. He told me that he's all done watching his good money go to waste. It's time for you to go upstairs and learn from the other girls about how to take "proper care" of his customers."

August's heart was pounding against her rib cage. "Oh, Ms. Rosa! I can't, I just can't! Please let me stay here with you. Can't you talk to Sal again and tell him how much help I am to you down here in the kitchen? Maybe if he knows that, he'll let me stay and help you?"

"Oh dear girl, you must know that I tried that. I gave it my best shot, but like I told you earlier, he's a stubborn, determined man. His mind gets set on something and he's not bound to change it. Not for me. Not for nobody."

August laid her folded arms on the table and let her head drop on top of them. As if hiding her face and her tears would make it somehow hurt less. She wished that were possible, although she knew it was not. If it were, the pain in her chest wouldn't feel like her heart was shriveling up and dying at that very moment.

"I won't go up there, Ms. Rosa. I don't know what I'll do, but I can't go up there! I won't, even for one minute, learn how to properly serve drinks to drunk people while wearing nothing but undergarments!"

"I know. I know. I'm still trying to work out something. There's *got* to be something I can do. If there is any way I can help you from being one of "those girls," I will. You've got to trust me on that."

August did trust her. She had no reason not to. Rosa had only ever been kind and protective of her since she had first laid eyes on her. She could see that Rosa wanted badly to help but August was also old enough to see that Rosa was a little old lady and certainly no match for the likes of that evil man, Sal. As tough and determined as she may be, Sal was pure evil.

"Thank you for looking out for me. I think you must be an angel sent straight from heaven. Sent just for me."

Rosa smiled. "Thank you, sweet girl. Truth is, if I were an angel, I wouldn't be working down in this kitchen with an illegal booze joint doing business upstairs. If I were an angel, neither you nor I would be in this kitchen right now trying to figure out a way to get you away from a life of indecency."

"*You* aren't doing anything wrong, Rosa. All you do is cook food. I don't think that's against the law in anybody's mind."

"Just the same. Being here *is* against the law. If the police ever raided the place, I'd be thrown in the clinker just the same as anyone gambling and drinking upstairs."

August thought about what Rosa said and decided that it wasn't fair. Rosa was a good woman. She had no choice but to work in the kitchen after her husband died. She wanted to believe that the law would understand that if they were to ever come in to shut the place down. John Finnegan was a much bigger outlaw than Ms. Rosa could ever be. An outlaw who was no doubt, at that very minute, driving from state-to-state smuggling liquor into places just like Sal's illegal juke joint. After what he'd done to August, part of her (a large part) wished that he'd get caught because it's what he deserved. He should be thrown in jail and left there to rot just as he had left her to do with Sal.

Rosa began to speak after a few minutes of complete silence. "The good news is that we still have two more days before Sal expects you upstairs. That's two extra days that I'll have time to think and see what I can come up with."

August lifted her face that was now red, swollen and soaked with tears. "I sure hope you can figure out something. I can't do what he wants. I just can't. I'd rather be dead."

"Hush now. Don't say things like that. I'm still trying to hatch a plan. I didn't expect to have to lay out an escape this soon, but now that I know better, I'll have to work faster and see what I can figure out. No more talk about wanting to be dead though. I won't have that, young lady. I just won't. Are we clear?"

"Yes Ma'am. I understand. What about if you just show me the way out of here and I can run away when it's dark outside? In the dark of night, no one will see me. That could work, couldn't it?"

"And go where? You can't go running off into the dark of night with no place to go. It's not safe out there in this city. Chicago is full of criminals."

August piped up, "It's not safe *inside* with Sal either. That man gives me the willies."

That evening, after the kitchen chores were all done, Rosa sat beside her as August laid on the cot. Since that first night when the screaming young girl had come to her kitchen, Rosa hadn't left to go to her own home. Not once. Every night she stayed right there in the kitchen, where she spent her days cooking, refusing to leave and give anyone an opportunity to grab the girl from her care.

Tired as she was, August couldn't sleep with so much on her mind. She kept thinking of random questions that plagued her mind. Though Rosa had told her more than once that it was time to sleep, she kept answering the young girl the best way she knew how. Rosa understood that August was anxious and scared half to death. Trying to find an explanation for "Why is the sky blue?" or "Why don't the clouds fall to the ground?" were things that kept the child's mind off some very adult like problems that neither of them wanted to think about. For a few minutes, which turned into hours, they pushed the real world outside the kitchen doors, aside. In their hearts, they both wished there were some way to forget those problems altogether. Even as a young girl, August understood that it was a childish, unrealistic thing to expect. Her childhood days were about over, and she would have done anything to stop that from happening. Her father had stolen those days from her the day he left her to fend for herself with a thug named Sal.

CHAPTER NINE

The next morning, August woke to Rosa gently shaking her shoulders. "You don't need to get up yet. I just wanted to tell you that I need to go out. I've got to run home for a minute, but I'll be back before you know it."

August opened her eyes but couldn't keep them open long. In seconds, she was asleep again. When she finally woke up, it was the sound of sizzling bacon that told her growling stomach it was time to get up.

"Good morning, Rosa. Was I dreaming or did you tell me that you were going to go home?"

Rosa smiled. "That was not a dream, my dear. I went home but it was only for a split second and then I hurried back."

Over breakfast, Rosa explained how she'd been working on a plan. A plan that would hopefully keep her from being forced to go on display in undergarments for wealthy drunks to ogle at and paw after. August could barely contain her excitement as she shoved pieces of crispy bacon into her mouth.

"Please tell me *all* about it, what's the plan? How do I get away from Sal?"

"Well, it's not an easy thing to do. I can tell you that. Sal's reach is everywhere. Far and wide and not just in this city. He's got eyes everywhere."

"Then how will I ever get away from here? From him?" she cried.

"Well, that's why I left this morning. There's a woman from my neighborhood. I went to see her. This woman has been known to keep a secret or two in her day. And there's not a whole lot on the illegal side of life that she's not done a time or two."

"She sounds like Sal."

Rosa nodded her head. "Cut from the same cloth, those two. Although, she has a little more heart and a smidgeon of honesty that Sal doesn't. She isn't known for blackmailing her friends and acquaintances, either. Although she's not what anyone would call innocent, by any means."

"And this woman has agreed to help?"

"She has. Seems Sal double crossed her a few years back. She jumped at the chance to pay him back his due, which is some real good fortune shining down on us."

For the first time in days, August was beginning to

THE ROAD TO MARIETTA

feel a spark of hope. Maybe she really *could* get away from Sal and his awful plan to turn her into some sort of barmaid or as Ms. Rosa called them, "jezebels in heels". She was willing to take any chance she had to take if it meant getting away.

"When do I leave? What do I have to do?"

Rosa laughed. "Now, hold on a minute. As I said, it's not going to be an easy thing to do. It will be dangerous and scary at times. I wish I could go with you, but I can't. Sal's got his finger on me hard, as you know. He's got eyes watching me and my every move, same as he does for everyone that works for him. That's why I met my "friend" at my house today. Sal knows I need to go home every now and again so he wouldn't think anything was amiss if his goons saw me go there."

August knew it was true that Rosa wasn't treated well or trusted by Sal. He wasn't the type to trust *anybody*, even the old lady in the basement who cooked his meals. August knew it would be hard to leave Rosa behind but there was no other way. Stay and be enslaved for life or make a run for it. Those were her options. No matter what the second option entailed, she was taking it. That much she knew for sure. August could see the look of concern on Rosa's furrowed brow and knew that even the adult in the room was worried about the plan she'd come up with.

"Whatever you tell me to do, I'll do it. Whatever needs to be done for me to get away from here, I can do. I know I'm just a kid, but I feel like I've had to grow up quick in the past few weeks. I can do this. I know I can. It doesn't matter how dangerous or scary the plan is, I'll do it. I will."

Rosa reached for her hand and held it. She didn't speak a single word, yet August heard an entire conversation in the silence. After a few minutes, she began to lay out the details of a very roughly planned escape.

"Few people know it, but this building has a secret tunnel underneath it. The tunnel connects to the church next door. I've heard about it, but I've never seen it, even though it's on the same floor as the kitchen we are in right now. I've heard that Sal stores his liquor in the church basement at the end of the tunnel. I hate to say it but it's brilliant, really. The cops would never go looking for liquor in a church basement. In exchange for the pastor's silence and the storage space, Sal donates a very hefty sum of money, anonymously, of course, to the church."

"A generous criminal." August chided.

"The thing is there's always a man guarding the entrance to the tunnel. An armed man, August. You'll need to go through when he's not there. Trouble is, he's *always* there. I'm working on a plan to divert him long enough for you to get past."

Suddenly August understood why Rosa was concerned about her safety. She was a young girl; how could she be a match for a grown man with a gun? Her heart began to beat faster as she realized that she had been living, working, and sleeping for the past few weeks, right down the hall from a man whose job was to stand guard with a loaded gun. She was suddenly grateful that she wasn't a sleepwalker.

She also understood, more than she had before, the type of dangerous place in which she'd been left. The kind of place children should never be. And yet, it was exactly the kind of place that her father thought to be a perfectly acceptable place to dump her. He knew what those people were like and yet he took the money and ran without once looking back.

Cold chills ran up and down her spine as she thought of all the terrible things that could have happened to her already, if not for Rosa.

"How are you planning to distract an armed man and not get yourself killed?"

Rosa looked away staring at the stove across the room with deep intent. "That my dear, girl, I don't yet know. But I will. You need to get out of here before Sal gets his hands on you. There is no other choice that I can see. One way or another, I'll make damned sure that it works."

August smiled because she believed her. She took comfort in knowing that when Rosa said she would do something, there wasn't a question as to if it would get done or not. Her life was in the hands of a gray-haired elderly woman, and she couldn't have felt any safer.

CHAPTER TEN

Two days later, in the middle of the night, Rosa shook her awake. "It's time, sweet girl." was all she said.

August wiped the sleep from her eyes as she reached for the dress that laid across the foot of the bed. She threw it over her head and slipped on her ratty sneakers. She sat for a minute on the edge of the cot and looked around the room trying to take a mental snapshot of her surroundings. It hadn't been much, just a curtained off cubbyhole in the kitchen, but she'd been safe there and cared for. She would miss the clanging of pots and pans each morning telling her it was time to get up. It was a bittersweet day for sure. She wanted nothing more than to be free from the things that went on at Sal's club and at the same time, leaving Sal also meant that she would be leaving Rosa. What would happen to her when Sal found out that she'd helped August escape? He was a cold-hearted bully, and would no doubt punish her for losing his "property" When she'd asked, Rosa smiled and said, "Don't you worry yourself about Ms. Rosa. I've seen a thing or two in this world and lived through more than a few tough times. This won't be no exception. Just another chapter in the book of life to get through is all."

Still, August *would* worry because she knew Sal was a nasty, vengeful man who would never let betrayal go without severe punishment. The man had bought a human being, a child at that, without so much as the blink of an eye. Chances were he wouldn't hesitate when it came to hurting a defenseless old woman either.

Rosa put two dresses in a carpet bag along with two meat sandwiches made from leftover roast and biscuits. "You'll find some of those Snicker Doodle cookies you like so much in there too."

August smiled. Rosa had thought of everything. She had taken such good care of her since the first day she'd met her.

"Will I ever see you again?" she asked with tears in her eyes.

Rosa put her hand on August's head. As she smoothed her hair with one hand, she rested the other on the girls shoulder. "Now, now. Let's not worry about that now. We have so many more important things to worry about today, now don't we?"

August nodded. She knew Rosa was right. Part of her was terrified to leave the safety of the kitchen and yet another part of her was excited for the adventure that lie ahead.

"The first part of the plan is the armed guard. I'm going to convince him to come into the kitchen for a home cooked meal. I'm counting on him agreeing. It's the middle of the night and there are no customers upstairs, so it should be a suitable time to talk him into leaving his post. In the meantime, you are going to slip into the closet just outside this kitchen. There's mops, brooms, buckets, and cleaning supplies in there so you'll have to be extra careful not to knock anything over. Once inside, you will shut the door and stand *perfectly* still. As still as a board. Don't so much as breathe loud enough for him to hear you. I'll stop right outside the closet door to ask him if he enjoys apple pie. Then I'll continue to the kitchen with him. That's when you'll count quietly to one hundred and then run as fast as you can. Don't you dare look back or hesitate for even one second. You are hearing me child?"

"I hear you. How do you know he will be hungry? Won't he think it's odd that you never asked him to eat with you before now?"

Rosa smiled. "Well, a little birdie told me that he has a soft spot for biscuits and sausage gravy. Just so happens to be what I've got on the stove as we speak." She winked and August smiled. Rosa looked proud of herself for coming up with the plan. She'd worked

THE ROAD TO MARIETTA

hard with little sleep as of late and August knew that. No amount of thanks would ever be enough, and she knew that too.

Once she was through the tunnel and outside of the church, she was to run directly to the library one block away. There she would be met by Rosa's friend Esther, who would be waiting for her at the back steps. Esther would take her in a farm truck, a few towns over to a train station. There, she would catch a train bound for a town called Garner. According to Rosa, Garner, was nothing but a pin dot on a map. She would get off the train and wait for a young man named Caleb to pick her up and take her to his family home. There she could stay for as long as she needed or wanted.

August knew nothing about any of those people, but she trusted Rosa to do the right thing by her. Also, she didn't have a whole lot of choices. If she couldn't put her trust and faith in the woman who had been so kind to her, then who could she trust? Not to mention the fact that without Rosa's plan, she would have no choice but to go to work for Sal.

August reached for her only friend in the entire world and clung to her like there was no tomorrow. Truth was, there very well might not be if she was to get caught trying to escape. Rosa wrapped her arms around August and gave her a long, tight squeeze.

"Don't be frightened, child. You are a brave, brave girl. You can do this, and I know that in my heart. If I didn't think so, I wouldn't be letting you take a risk like this. I've seen your bravery and determination. I know you will follow my instructions to a "T" and be free of this place before your life goes in a bad direction."

The faith she had in August gave her courage. She felt herself stand a little taller as Rosa spoke. August *had* learned to be brave out of necessity and it was time for her to draw from that part of her soul again. Her life was depending on it. Rosa pulled away from her and held her by the shoulders, looking her directly in the eyes.

"You can do this. I want you to be free and happy. Remember this place and steer clear of people like them wherever you go. I will never forget you child. I know you will go and make something of yourself out there in this world. It's time now. It's time for you to go."

August felt a tight lump in her throat as she told her how much she appreciated everything she had done for her. Rosa didn't try to hide the flow of tears that silently rolled down her cheeks.

"I'll never, ever forget you either, Ms. Rosa. I promise."

August closed her eyes, inhaled as deeply as she could and calmly said, "Okay, I'm ready now."

CHAPTER ELEVEN

Rosa took her hand as they entered the dark hallway and arrived at the broom closet. She squeezed August's hand and whispered into her ear, "Live free and fly high out there, child. You will be with me forever." She handed her a box of wooden matches and waited as she stepped inside the closet.

August closed the door behind her after she'd entered the tiny dark space. She was sure that her pounding heart was about to jump right out of her chest. *"Don't move a muscle. Try not to breathe too loud."* she repeatedly told herself. She prayed that the echo of her heart, beating like a drumline, would not be heard by anyone but her. The pulsating in her ears was almost deafening.

She strained to listen for the sound of movement in the dark hallway. A door made from flimsy wood was all that stood between her safety and getting grabbed or even killed by a goon with a gun. Realizing this made her hands shake and droplets of sweat trickle down her forehead.

There was no sound at all in the hallway for what seemed like forever. No voices. No footsteps. Nothing. Had something gone wrong with Rosa's plan? Maybe she couldn't persuade the guard to follow her to the kitchen? Every possible scenario ran through her head as she stood statue still behind the wooden door. Droplets of sweat poured down her nose and pooled on the front of her dress. August let them fall. She was too afraid she would knock something over if she tried to move her hand to wipe her forehead. She was about to run for her life far away from a horrible, sleezy man. She figured she could deal with a little sweat in her eyes. If that were as bad as things got during her escape, she knew she'd be fine.

As time crawled on in complete silence, the stillness was beginning to turn her fear into sheer agitation. Where was Rosa? Where was the guard? What was going on outside of the broom closet? The longer she listened to the sound of silence, the more she worried. She understood clearly what would happen to her if anyone were to find her. She had a real good idea what would happen to Rosa too. Neither situation would be good for either of them. If something were to happen to Rosa because of her, August would never be able to live with herself. She was certain that if Sal got his hands on Rosa, her punishment would be so much worse than her own. He had paid her father good money for her because she could make him *more* money. But Rosa, was the old woman who cooked for Sal and his customers, he could replace her in a second. For the safety of both, August kept her breath to a slow murmur and continued to stay perfectly still.

Finally, she heard voices. They were further down the hall, but there were definitely voices echoing through the hall. As they drew closer, she could hear a man talking a mile a minute and even stop to laugh aloud a time or two. She also heard Rosa laughing and joking. Rosa was laying on the charm as she told the guard how she worked all day in the kitchen baking biscuits and sausage gravy but didn't have anyone to share it with. He was pleased that she thought to ask him to join her because it just so happened that it was his favorite meal.

August heard them walking slowly toward the kitchen stopping every now and again to chat. She heard them linger right outside the door as Rosa offered him pie after dinner. The guard jumped at the invitation. At that moment, August began to slowly count to one hundred just as she was instructed to do. She had to pace herself, so she didn't count too fast and leave the closet too soon. She reached one hundred just like Rosa had said to do. Finally it was time to make her escape. She reached for the door and realized that her hand was shaking in time with her racing heartbeat. *"Breathe, August. Just breathe."* she reminded herself. She inhaled, took a deep breath, and silently exhaled. She pushed the closet door open in slow motion. When it was cracked enough for her to fit through the opening, August took one final deep breath and stepped out of her refuge and into the hall.

She could smell Rosa's cooking from where she stood. She would miss those meals. She would miss Rosa too. But this was her shot at freedom, and she had to take it. Thanks to her father, who hadn't given a tinker's dam what happened to her, it was up to *her* to find her way to safety.

She put one foot in front of the other and willed her legs to follow. The tunnel, like the closet was also filled with pure darkness so she lit a match to light the way. August slowly closed the door behind her and knew that it was time to go. When the match burned out, she hugged the wall to find her way instead of lighting another match that she may need later.

Rosa had instructed her to keep going and stop only when she reached the end where she would find a door. One of Rosa's "little birdies" supplied information about a hidden key tucked into a crack on top of the door frame. When she reached the door, she stood on her tip toes and ran her fingers along the frame until she felt the cold metal skeleton key in her sweaty, shaking hand. *"Don't drop it!"* she ordered herself silently. The sound of metal on the cement floor would sound like a giant rock being tossed down the tunnel.

She grasped the key tightly in her fingers and unlocked the door. She returned the key to its hiding spot and walked into another room that she hoped was the church basement. The cool, musty odor hit her in the face as soon as she opened the door. The room was as black as a boot. She lit another match and was quickly taken aback by the number of wooden crates stacked from floor to ceiling. There was only a narrow path through the middle of the room. The entire basement looked like a maze of moonshine. When she'd made her way through, she reached another door. As she reached for the latch, she could hear voices on the other side. Her heart raced. Rosa hadn't said anything about the possibility of someone being in the church basement. She didn't know what else to do but crouch behind the tallest stack of crates. She blew out the match and prayed that she wouldn't be discovered.

The heavy wooden door creaked loudly as it slowly opened. She made herself as small as she could behind the crates at the far end of the room and held her breath. Two people were there in the basement with her.

"Put the cases of candles over there. Just on top of that stack of crates to the left, young man. Best for everyone if no one knows what's in those boxes. You understand what I'm saying?"

A boy's voice echoed, filling the room with his words. "Yes, sir. I understand."

"Good. Set those candles down and remember that you were never here."

"Yes, Pastor Dailey."

Seconds later, the door closed. August

continued to sit perfectly still in the dark. Although Rosa told her all about the church and how they were hiding Sal's moonshine for him, she hadn't wanted to believe that a church would really have dealings with a criminal like Sal. It didn't matter if she believed it or not, the proof was there in front of her very own eyes. The money Sal donated to the church must have been exceptionally large. Large enough that they couldn't turn down his offer, was all she could figure.

Just as she'd done before in the broom closet, she slowly counted to one hundred to give the men time to get away from the basement door before she opened it. When she'd done that, she stood and reached for the handle once again, praying the entire time that she had counted slowly enough.

CHAPTER TWELVE

August stepped out into a small hallway with six steps in front of her. Six steps. That was all that stood between her being forced to be a hootchie girl for Sal and freedom. She stood and stared at the steps in front of her, like it was the first time she'd ever seen stairs. As soon as she found a door leading outside she would run like the devil himself was chasing after her.

There was light shining into the hall from the colorful stained-glass windows high above. She was grateful for the sound of absolute silence. Now all she had to do was climb those six steps and find the exit. Then she would run to the library and meet Esther. August had no idea what she looked like, but Ms. Rosa said she wouldn't be able to miss her. She'd told her how her friend kind of "stood out" because she liked to wear men's overall's and a bright orange hat everywhere she went. Esther sounded to August like a character in a book from a dime store, she had read once.

She tip toed up the stairs and pushed open the door to the outside and ran as fast as her feet would carry her, letting the heavy door swing closed behind her. Just as Rosa had said, the library was within view. It was a small brick building with white trim and long, tall windows that reached from floor to ceiling.

When she'd reached the large granite steps, she sat down to pray silently to a God she wasn't sure she even believed in yet. She prayed that neither Sal nor his goons would see her sitting out there in broad daylight. Someone "up there" must have been listening because she hadn't even sat for five minutes when an old farm truck pulled up, driven by a woman in a bright orange hat.

"You must be August?" she asked.

"You must be Esther?"

"One and only. C'mon child, climb aboard and let's leave some dust in the ole rearview if you know what I mean." She laughed.

August went around the truck to the passenger side and climbed in. It was not much to look at, but it was an automobile that worked. The outside had more rust on it than color, but here and there she could see faded patches of red paint. Inside, the seats were torn. Black tape stretched tight in a tic tac toe pattern to hold the seat together. She could feel the stickiness of the tape against her legs as she sat but she wasn't about to complain about a little thing like that. She was grateful for the help.

Rosa had described Esther perfectly. She did indeed wear men's overalls and men's boots too. The bright orange hat on her head should have looked ridiculous on a woman, but it did not. Somehow, it all worked perfectly well with the build of this woman. Lit cigarette in hand, she was quite a character August decided.

Esther noticed August sizing her up. She looked at the girl out of the corner of her eye as she drove.

"Guessin' you ain't never come across a lady wearin' fellas clothes before?"

August didn't say a word. She continued to stare out the window.

"Oh, hey. It's okay. I don't take offense to anybody takin' a second look my way. I never did care much for the frilly girl look and to be honest with ya, there just ain't nothing anymore comfy than a good ole pair of men's overalls."

When she smiled, August could see the dark spaces where teeth used to be but were not any longer. Blondish curly hair stuck out where it wasn't being smushed down by the weight of her hat. They weren't the loose, pretty curls like August had seen on some women. This woman's hair looked more like tightly woven fibers of steel wool.

Esther had a smile on her face that seemed to have no beginning or end. It stretched completely across the woman's face. August decided she liked her bubbly personality. Yes. Esther might be someone she could like.

"You know where you're heading to?"

August shrugged. "No, not really. I mean, Rosa told me you were taking me to a train station a few towns over."

"Where ya from kid?"

August didn't know how to answer that. "Nowhere in particular."

Esther laughed. "Aww c'mon now, everybody's from somewhere."

August answered with a tone that was a bit snappier than she'd meant it to be. "Well, *everybody* isn't because I'm *somebody* and I'm not from anywhere in particular!"

"Hey now! Settle down. I didn't mean to rustle your feathers or nothin.' I was just curious."

August felt bad that her voice had risen loudly without meaning for it to. She opened her mouth, and it was as though she didn't have any say in the matter. Her tongue had run away on its own. The woman was trying to be polite and make conversation with her and she'd made her feel bad. Now she felt bad too.

August hung her head. "I'm sorry. I didn't mean to bite your head off like that. Truth is that I don't know where I'm from. I lived most of my life with my father. He was a traveling salesman. We went a lot of places but never stayed anywhere too long."

"I see. Well, that's okay. You've seen a lot of places then. That's a good thing. Most folks can't say that, but you can." she grinned.

"We rode *through* a lot of states, but I can't say I ever really saw too much of any of them. What I could see out the window was about it."

"Where's your Ma?"

August went back to looking out the window. "Died giving birth to me is what I was told."

"That so? Well, I'd say a new adventure is just what a girl like you needs."

The gears of the old jalopy made a grinding noise every so often followed by a rocking of the truck cab that about tossed them from one side to the other.

"We got us about a half day's ride to the town where the train station is. I made us a little lunch from a leftover ham. Couple of sandwiches here in the sack. A cookie or two in there too. You just help yourself whenever you want, Ms. August."

August was starving. Even though she had her own leftovers in her bag, she had no idea what may lie ahead for her. She would hold onto the lunch Rosa send with her just in case she couldn't find food for a few days. She was good and hungry though. She could have eaten every crumb of food in the burlap bag on the seat between them. But she didn't let on. She didn't want to come across as a beggar or greedy, so she waited. When Esther was hungry, she'd eat too and not before. But just knowing there was ham inside that sack, made her stomach churn, and start growling. Loudly. August hoped Esther couldn't hear it too.

As they drove, she told August all about how she lived on the same farm for her entire life. She said she'd had dreams of running off to Hollywood where she would become a famous actress. She explained all about how her brother had left the farm and set out for California, but he'd gotten sick along the way and died. Esther had to stay on the farm and work with her Ma and Pa. She said she hadn't minded giving up on her dreams because her mother and father had given up their lives for her and her brother. She proudly talked about how family takes care of family, even if it meant changing plans for a life's dream.

August couldn't even begin to imagine what it would feel like to know that kind of love from a parent, let alone two. Esther said there was another sister, Arlene but she didn't say anything much about her. August felt like there was a lot more that Esther could tell her about her sister but wasn't going to. According to Rosa, Arlene had quite a "colorful" past and she figured that's why Esther didn't really want to talk much about her.

She wondered how Esther knew Rosa, and she planned to ask when she could get a word in edgewise. August had never quite known anyone who liked to talk as much as Esther. The first chance she got, she blurted out, "How do you know Rosa?"

"Rosa? Oh, I've known her all my life. She's a peach ain't she?"

"A peach?" August asked unsure of what that meant.

"You know, a sweet person. She and my sister, Arlene are friendly. She lives in Rosa's neighborhood, right down the street from one another, I hear. I don't really visit over at Arlene's too often. I've known Rosa all my life, though. She was born and brought up right down the road from us on her folk's farm."

"Ms. Rosa grew up on a farm?"

"She sure did. Their family farm is still there. Of course, it's not *their* farm anymore but it's still right there, down the road from ours. Her parents passed away and she couldn't keep the place up. It all ended up going to the bank once the depression came. So many farms just like theirs have gone belly up during this tough time."

August wasn't sure what the "depression" was all about either. She'd read the word in the newspaper, and she'd heard it spoken on the radio, but she really didn't understand what it meant.

"What exactly does that mean? The *depression*? I've heard that word before in the newspaper and on the radio, but I don't know what it's all about. Do you?"

Esther waved her hand into the air dismissively. "Oh, it's one of them fancy government words that means there's no money and the country's gone broke. Ain't nobody 'round with money. Not the government and surely not regular folks like us. Nobody has it. And there ain't jobs for folks to work at to make any money."

August decided that Esther was a whole lot smarter than she looked. Although she didn't have the faintest idea how a whole country could go broke, she did know firsthand what it meant to be poor. She couldn't count the times her father had told her that she couldn't have a candy bar at a gas station or a meal at a diner because they were flat broke, and that he "wasn't made of money." The older she grew, she understood how "broke" to him really meant they didn't have money for anything *she* wanted. Except when it came to cigarettes and new suits, he'd sure found the money somewhere. Evidently a man can sell more bootleg liquor if he wears a suit.

"Say, you want to grab us a sandwich out of that sack? I haven't eaten since breakfast and my stomach is downright angry about it."

August was so relieved that Esther was hungry too. Her stomach had gone way past hungry and was teetering on a painful hurt. She reached in the bag and took a sandwich out for each of them. She knew before she even tasted the food, that she could have eaten everything in that sack all on her own.

Esther was halfway through hers when she looked over at August and smiled. "Either I made a darned good ham, or you got yourself a powerful hunger today, young lady. Good! I'm glad to see it. Reach right on in there and grab another. I made a few up for us just in case."

August felt herself blushing and wishing she hadn't wolfed the first one down so fast. But she couldn't' help it. It was good and she was starving. She should have been accustomed to a growling stomach by now. She'd gone longer stretches without food while traveling with her father. She realized at that moment, how quickly she'd become accustomed to eating on a regular basis back in Rosa's kitchen. She tried to eat the second sandwich slower but before she knew it, it too was gone. Her eyes began to get heavy as she listened to Esther talking about how the depression had affected her family and their farm, along with most of the people in town. August leaned against the door and felt the cool of the window against her cheek as they bounced around the cab of the truck. Hitting a pothole in the road threw them clear into the air, but somehow Esther managed to keep ahold of the steering wheel. Once the truck was steadily moving down the road again, August felt her eyelids grow heavy.

When Esther shook her awake, they had reached their stop. "This is it, child. This here's where you need to be."

"We're there already?" August asked, wiping the sleep from her eyes. "I thought we had hours to go."

Esther laughed as she shut off the ignition. "Well that was a few hours back. You slept the last few miles away."

She hadn't meant to sleep. She'd tried to keep her eyes open so she could see where it was that she'd be going.

"Where are we?"

"At the train station, child. You'll take these coins and go to that booth for a ticket bound for Garner. The ticket master will give you a ticket so you can board the train."

August hadn't realized she would need money to ride a train. "Thank you, Esther. One day I will repay you for your kindness and for the ticket money. I promise I will."

"Oh never you mind about that. Rosa's a good friend and I was glad to help. Besides, you can thank her for the ticket money. She arranged all of that for you. She sure must think the world of you, young lady. Times being so hard as they are and all, she made darned sure you had train fare."

August smiled. "She's a special lady. The best person I've ever known. You are nice too, Esther. I'm thankful for your help in getting me away from…well, away from *that* place.

Esther laid her hand on August's shoulder. "Think nothin' of it. Now, you best get going. You don't want to miss that train."

She got out of the truck, walked August to the platform, and gave her a hug. "No matter where you end up in this life, know that Ms. Rosa, and me too, will always keep you in our thoughts and prayers Ms. August."

August smiled back at her and walked to the window. Once she had a ticket in her hand giving her passage to Garner, she looked back to see Esther waving from the cab of her truck as she drove off leaving a cloud of dust and smoke behind her. It was just her now. Just her and a big ole steel train about to take her to a town she'd never heard of to meet another person she didn't know. She was nervous but knew she could do it. She had to. Rosa had gone over and above to make sure she got away from Sal, and she wasn't about to let her down.

CHAPTER THIRTEEN

The train car was only about half full, with plenty of seats to choose from. August sat near the front, across from an older woman doing needlework. She wore a flowered dress and a green jacket, along with a matching hat. August suddenly felt self-conscious of her own clothing.

She tried to smooth the wrinkles from her dress and sat the bag Rosa had given her on the seat next to her. A man in a blue uniform and a square top hat walked down the aisle, stopping to greet each passenger and collect their tickets. August's thoughts went to Rosa as she handed him hers. There she was, working for Sal, making mere pennies for all the demanding work she did. Yet she used her hard-earned money to get a ticket for August, a girl she had only known for a few weeks. She felt so fortunate to be there on that train at that moment.

Once the tickets had been collected, the conductor stood at the front of the car and called out, "Train's leaving now folks. Settle in. First stop will be Garner about two hours down the line. The next car back has coffee, soft drinks, and baked items for sale if you're interested."

August didn't know what she was supposed to do for the next two hours. In the backseat of her daddy's car, she'd had books and newspapers to read. That always made the time go faster. She didn't have any of that with her now.

The train pulled out of the station, and she sat glued to the window watching the scenery pass by. She'd traveled a lot of places in her young life, but she realized it wasn't the same. What she was seeing from the window of the train was nothing like what she'd seen from the car window. The views of plush green trees and mountains fascinated her. Even the tall swaying grasses of the fields looked different from the view of the train. She realized then that trains could go through countryside's that cars never could because there were no roads, only steel tracks.

The people she saw passing by the window were different too. Barefoot children yelling and waving at the train as it passed by them. The makeshift houses seemed to be made of nothing more than scraps of wood and tin from what she could see. She'd never seen so many little shacks gathered close together like that.

Miles and miles of watching trees pass by made her eyes tired. The rocking motion of the train and constant rhythm of the wheels lulled her off to sleep, once again.

"Excuse me, Miss? Would you be interested in a soft drink?"

It was the older woman sitting across the aisle from her. She thought hard as to how she should answer. She would have loved a soft drink but the only money she had, was given to the ticket master back at the station. August wondered if the woman could tell she didn't have a penny to her name because she didn't wait for an answer.

The woman spoke up, "Of course, I'd be honored if you'd allow me to pay. I have this bit of money in my pocket just burning a hole."

August smiled. "Really? That's so nice of you ma'am."

"Please call me Irene. Ma'am sounds much too old. Would you like a cola?"

"Yes, please. A cold cola would be wonderful."

"My pleasure young lady. What do they call you, Miss?"

"August. My name is August."

"Well, it's a pleasure to meet you Ms. August. I'll just be a minute. Do me good to stretch my legs. I'll be back in two shakes of a lambs tail."

August thought of Ms. Rosa as Irene walked away. She had never imagined there were so many kind people in the world. According to her Daddy, the world was filled with terrible people but that was not the experience she was having. Somehow, it had been her good fortune to meet at least two of the good ones.

Irene returned with a soft drink for August and a cup of tea for herself. "Thank you again." August said as she raised the bottle to her parched lips.

Irene smiled. "Do you mind if I ask you a question? Why is it that you are traveling alone?"

August was caught off guard by the question. What was she supposed to say? She certainly couldn't tell her the truth.

"I'm going to see a friend. A friend of the family. My Mama had to stay at home with the other kids and couldn't come with me. Still, she really wanted me to see her friend over in Garner. I told her it was fine. I'm more than old enough to travel alone." It scared August how quickly the lie had come out of her mouth with truly no effort. She decided that later, when life settled down for her, she'd have to work on that. She didn't want to be a liar. She appreciated when people told her the truth and she always wanted to do the same for anyone she spoke to. But at that moment, she didn't see any other option. Life had become about survival. She would ask for forgiveness later once she decided who it was that she should be asking.

Irene nodded her head. "I see. I'm from Garner too so I guess we're going to the same place. I wonder if I might know your family friend?"

August's heart raced and she knew her face must have been burning because she felt her cheeks getting warmer. She was praying that Irene couldn't see her discomfort as well.

"No. I mean, probably not. They only moved there a short time ago. Which is why I'm going. I'll be helping them unpack and stay for a while until they get settled in."

Irene smiled. "Isn't that nice of you. They are truly fortunate to have your help."

"Thank you. I'm really looking forward to spending time there."

The woman nodded and took a sip of the steaming hot tea. August's gut told her that she wasn't believing a single word of what August had just rattled off. And that was okay. As soon as the train stopped and the passengers exited, she would never see the woman again. Why *should* the woman believe her anyhow since it was all a big ole steaming heap of lies? She just hadn't known what else to say.

Her explanation sounded better than the truth. The truth being that she had no idea where she was going or who she was meeting in Garner. Whoever August was meeting, she hoped they were good people like Rosa and Esther. The thought of being led somewhere by yet another stranger made her stomach squirm. She had no choice but to trust that the plan was for her to be somewhere safe.

"You said you were going back home to Garner. Have you been gone long?"

Irene smiled. "Yes. My daughter lives in Springtown and she had a baby recently. I've been staying with her family and helping with the new baby for the past month or so."

August smiled. She could tell that Irene was probably a good mother and grandmother.

"Babies are nice." was all August could come up with. What did she know about babies? She'd never even held one before.

"Oh, they certainly are. Especially when they are your grandbabies to spoil like the dickens"

Irene went on and on talking about her daughter and son- in -law, who were corn farmers. They were doing well despite the economy being so tough. "No matter what the world looks like, people still need corn. Animals need it too."

Irene also had a son who lived in Garner. He and his wife hadn't *yet* been blessed by the Good Lord and given children, but she prayed daily for that to happen anytime.

The conductor stood in the front of the car and yelled out to the passengers. "Garner station just ahead. Don't forget your belongings and wait for the train to make a complete stop before standing up."

August took a deep breath. This was it. This is where she would leave the safety of the train car and of her new acquaintance, Irene, bound for parts unknown once again. She felt her heart pounding with anxiousness. She'd been fortunate so far to have met some truly kind people along the way and had to blindly trust that it would be the same when she got off the train.

"Watch over me, Momma, will you please?" she asked silently as the train came to a stop.

Irene stood to exit and gave her a hug before she

stepped down from the train. "Safe travels Ms. August. May the Good Lord bless you in whatever you do and wherever you go."

She pressed a dollar into August's hand and closed her fingers around it.

August didn't understand. "But…"

"Just in case. You tuck that away just in case you ever need it. You hear?"

"Yes, Ms. Irene. Thank you." August replied as she hugged the woman back.

August grabbed her sorry looking bag that had seen better days and waited for the other passengers to leave the train before she got in line. All around her, people were running around in a frenzy. Everyone seemed to know where they were going and who they were meeting. Everyone but her. It didn't matter if she were last exiting the train because she had no idea about whom she was meeting or what would happen once she stepped foot onto the wooden platform beside the tracks.

CHAPTER FOURTEEN

The Garner stop was much bigger than the previous station had been. Crowds of people scurried around trying to find their loved ones who were exiting the train. August stood back and watched a family of six children run to the side of the train leaping into the arms of a man she guessed to be their father. She wondered what that would feel like. To be hugged for dear life by a parent was something she certainly had never known. She wondered if those children knew how lucky they were.

The *only* thing August knew at that moment was that she was supposed to meet someone named Caleb, though she wouldn't know him from a hole in the ground. He could have been any one of the people milling about the station and she wouldn't have known it. As it turned out, he wasn't. After an hour, about everyone had cleared out from the depot. Everyone but her. She sat on the wooden bench outside the ticket office. She couldn't go anywhere. She didn't know the first thing about this strange town she had arrived in.

After a while, she heard the pattering of running footsteps approaching the platform. A teenage boy approached her and took off his hat before he spoke.

"Miss? My name's Caleb. You wouldn't be August would you?"

August smiled. "I was hoping you'd be coming along soon."

"Sorry. Had a bit of trouble with the ole jalopy. She's mired back there a bit in the woods, but I thought I'd better start walking and come find you before you thought I'd forgotten all about you. We're gonna have to walk back a way to reach the truck. I'm real sorry about that Miss."

"That's okay. I don't mind walking."

He put his worn ball cap back on his head and placed his hands on his hips. His clothes were about as rag tag as her own. He wore a t-shirt that probably hadn't been white in a very long time. His blue jeans had more holes in them than not and were much too short for his legs. His boots matched her sneakers as they too were without laces. There was instantly something comfortable about him that helped her to feel more at ease than she had on the train. Maybe it was that he seemed closer to her own age or maybe it was because he looked as scruffy as she felt she did herself. Either way, there was a familiarity and comfort about him. A comfort that said she didn't need to prove anything to him. There was no need to feel self-conscious about being who she was, and it felt good to feel that way.

After he put his hat back on, he smoothed the loose blonde curls sticking out from under it and brushed the hair from his eyes. August couldn't help but notice his warm, soft smile. When he smiled, she felt suddenly warm and toasty as though she was snuggled in under a cozy blanket.

Right away, she could see that Caleb had a shyness about him. However, she could also sense that there was something about him that said he was quite capable of walking just this side of mischief. Immediately, August found him intriguing. She had a feeling in the pit of her stomach that told her he was like touching a hot stove that you *know* will burn you but watching your hand reach for the flame anyway.

"We ought to be getting back to the truck."

August stood to follow him. Though she didn't understand exactly what she was feeling or why, she had a feeling she would have followed him about anywhere.

"Do you have a bag? I'd be happy to carry it for you." he offered.

"No. I just have this old thing here. I got it but thank you anyway."

He started down the dirt road just past the train station and August followed. They walked in silence for a quite a while before he stopped and turned to her.

"Listen, I got some bad news. I'm not sure I will be able to get the stubborn ole mule of a truck unstuck. Not tonight anyway. Night is just around the corner. If I can't, we may have to stay the night right there. Soon it'll be too dark to walk the whole way home. I'm awfully sorry about this." He hung his head as he started walking away from her.

"That's okay." she assured him. "I don't mind. Not like I'm in any kind of hurry."

He asked where she was coming from. Once again August found herself wondering what she should say. She knew he was just trying to make small talk, just as Irene and Esther had done, but she still didn't know how to answer. She was ashamed that she was there in that moment because her father had sold her to a con man running an illegal speak easy. The rest of her story didn't exactly paint a pretty picture either.

She settled for keeping it as simple as she could and said that she'd come from Illinois and hoped he wouldn't press any further.

"Really? Never been there. I've never really been anywhere, other than Indiana."

August envied the fact that he had a place to call home. If she'd had a stable place to grow up, she would have gladly never gone anywhere else either. But she didn't. That was something she'd never known, and it sure looked like maybe she never would.

"You're not missing much." she muttered.

"I hear there's lots of excitement in Illinois and

lots to do. Always wanted to go. Especially to Chicago. Now *that* place sounds fun. I hear they don't even sleep at nighttime there. Can you imagine that?"

August didn't need to imagine. She'd seen it up close with her own eyes. She'd seen more of that city than she ever cared to see again.

"No kidding? Nah, I can't imagine that." she answered dryly.

"Around here they practically roll up the streets at the first sign of dusk. Wonder what it would be like in a big city like Chicago with all of them lights? Why, I bet there's dancing in the streets all night long."

Caleb looked at her for a reaction. She smiled and put Sal and her father and all that she'd been through to that point in her short life, in the back of her mind. *Way* in the back.

"Yeah. It's probably something to see, all right." she said in the most excited tone she could muster. Though her enthusiasm wasn't as wild as his, he seemed to believe she was as amazed as he was at the thought.

Light was disappearing quickly as they made their way up the road. Trees lined both sides of the dirt road. August was never fond of the darkness and thinking about what wandered around in the dark was beginning to give her the shivers.

"How much further to the truck? It's getting dark pretty quick."

Caleb laughed. "That's okay. I don't mind the dark. Do you?"

"Can't say it's my favorite thing in the world,

no."

"Why not? Ain't nothing different about the dark than the daytime. I work a lot of hours in the dark, so I'm used to it."

"You work? I mean, you have a job?"

"Sure. Lots of 'em. I work at the farm every day. All day. Sometimes I help other folks out with odd jobs when I can. Every dime helps. Or at least that's what Josie says."

"Josie?" August asked.

"Yeah. My sister, Josephine. We call her Josie for short. That's where we're going to whenever I can get that miserable heap unstuck. Out to our farm."

"Oh. I didn't know where we were going. I was just told to meet you at the station. Is she nice? Your sister?"

Caleb cocked his head. "Well, if you don't get on the wrong side of her she is. Make her mad and she turns into one ticked off rooster!"

August's eyes grew wide. "I'll remember that."

"Oh now, I didn't mean to scare you none. She's not too bad. She just has lots to do since Ma died is all. She does the best she can, I suppose."

"I'm sorry about your mother."

He was silent and said no more about his mother as he walked.

"What about your father? Where's he?"

Caleb chuckled. "Where's Pa? Well that's the million-dollar question. He ran off after Ma died. My little sister, Grace, was about six months old at the time. Said he wanted no part of raising kids on his own and he up and left."

August was sorry she asked. She could see that her question upset Caleb. "I'm sorry. That had to be hard on all of you."

She could see his defensive side kick in when he spat out, "Nah. Not me. Wasn't hard on me! I don't care if he's gone or not. I'm ashamed of him for high tailing it out and leaving Josie and I to do his job. If he had an ounce of decency he'd be ashamed of himself too, but he don't. It ain't right what he done. Truth is…I can't say I miss him."

August's heart felt heavy. This is where she was going to live? With a family that sounded like it had enough of its own troubles without throwing hers into the pot? She'd envisioned a place that wasn't merely about survival, but she could tell that this place she was following Caleb to, wasn't going to be it. Still, she knew that beggars couldn't be choosy. In her case, she was the beggar and she'd be grateful to them for taking her in, even if she had to sleep in a barn.

"Are you sure your sister wants another mouth to feed, Caleb? Sounds like you both have your hands full already."

"It's okay. We always got room for more. We know Rosa's sister and any friend of hers is a friend of ours. Besides, I'm sure she'll like having another girl around that's close to her age."

August was confused. "Your sister is *my* age?"

"Well I can't say for sure. You look to be what twelve? Maybe thirteen?"

August realized then that her thirteenth

birthday had come and gone while she had been with Rosa, and she had completely forgotten all about it. There had been more important things to worry about than a birthday.

"I'm thirteen."

He laughed. "I was close now wasn't I? Josie's fourteen and I'm fifteen."

"She's fourteen and raising your baby sister? *And* taking care of the farm?"

"That's not so unusual around here."

August didn't know what to say. She didn't realize that girls her age ran farms and raised babies, even if they were siblings.

They reached the truck and Caleb stopped the conversation. He wasn't kidding when he'd said the truck had been mired in the mud. Buried was more like it. The two back tires had all but disappeared. Dark, soupy mud had risen all the way up to the bottom of the doors.

"Holy cow!" she said in amazement. "Your truck *is* buried."

"You thought I was joking?" he smiled.

He stood with his hands on his hips surveying the predicament they were in. Every now and again he'd shake his head.

After a few minutes, August asked, "Come up with anything?"

"Huh? No. There's nothing to do but wait for daylight. We've had almost a month of rain around here. We never get that much rain, but we darn sure did this year. I hate to complain about it because we sure needed it. Haven't seen a drop in months and then all at once the heavy rains came, flooding everything. All we can hope for is that somebody comes along tonight and helps us get out of that hole. If not, come daylight I'll be able to see better and I'll find a way out."

"What will we do for tonight? I mean, where will we sleep?"

"You can take the cab and I'll curl up over at the tree line where it's drier."

August looked terrified. "What? You're not staying with me? You brought me out here in the middle of the boondocks and you're not going to stay with me?"

Caleb's face showed surprise at her outburst. "Alright. All right. You don't want me to leave you alone in the truck, I won't. I just thought you might not want to sleep with a stranger so close is all."

August hadn't even thought of that. Maybe it wasn't the best situation for a girl her age to find herself in, but she didn't care. Stranger or not, he was the only person she knew out there in the dark woods. Besides, he wasn't really a man. Still, even a boy of fifteen was more protection and security than none. It was so dark now that she couldn't see him if he were standing inches from her face. It was that dark. Anything could have been there that close to her, and she'd have not been able to see it. There was no way she was going to sleep in that truck alone.

"You'll behave yourself, won't you?" she asked timidly.

Caleb smiled. "Of course I will! Geeze! I just met you for cripes sake. I don't know what kind of guy you think I am but trust me when I tell you that you're safe with me."

August suddenly felt ashamed for thinking that Caleb was someone she had to fear. "I'm sorry. I didn't mean to offend you. I should have said that I'd really appreciate it if you stayed in the truck with me."

August sat on the passenger side of the rickety old truck and Caleb on the driver's side. Closing the doors hard behind them, shook the dead silence of the woods. The echo of the slamming doors must have been heard for a mile or more. She had never seen a forest that was so dark or heard a silence that was so loud.

"Are you hungry, Caleb? I got a couple of sandwiches in my bag that Rosa made this morning. I'm hungry and you must be too. Here, have a bite before we sleep."

She fished the sandwiches Rosa had sent her off with, out of her bag. They ate in silence until Caleb said, "Try to get some shut eye. I'm sure we'll get out of this mess tomorrow once day breaks."

"Goodnight, Caleb."

"Goodnight, August."

She pulled the collar of her dress snug around her neck and folded her arms in front of her. Her entire life she'd been sleeping in a vehicle. It was about as natural to her as breathing. Although she'd usually had the lights of passing cars or towns to lull her to sleep.

In what seemed like seconds, she heard the loud sound of Caleb snoring. For a boy his age, he was surprisingly as loud at sleeping as her father had been. Fortunately, August had learned to sleep well through her father sawing wood in his sleep.

CHAPTER FIFTEEN

Slowly shedding the sleep from her eyes, August could see that she was alone. A feeling of panic swept over her. Had this boy taken off and left her alone in the middle of nowhere? Why would he do that to her? Had she misjudged him when she'd decided he was safe to be alone with? She was quickly learning that a person could think they knew someone, but the truth was becoming vividly clear that one never really knows anyone but themself. You think someone cares about you and would never do anything to hurt you, and then they turn around sell you to a mobster like you are nothing but a piece of merchandise.

From the corner of her eye, she caught a flicker

of movement and turned to see Caleb slowly moving alongside the truck body. She felt relieved that he hadn't left her there alone and also a sense of relief that she hadn't misjudged him after all. He opened the driver's door and looked surprised to see that she was awake.

"Morning sleepyhead." he said with a sweet grin that washed a warmth over her body clear to her toes. Until the day before, she'd never known anyone to have such an effect on her. The wave of strange sensations exploded with a whoosh throughout her entire body. She didn't know what that was all about, but she liked it. She could feel her face begin to blush.

"Morning. I thought you left."

"What? And left you here alone in the middle of the woods?" he laughed. "You must *not* think very highly of me."

"No. It's not that. I just don't know you very well yet."

"Understood. I was just teasing you. I'm not offended. Truth is you *don't* know me, so I can't blame you for thinking something like that. Now that the suns coming up, I can see what we need to do to get us out of this mud. We'll need to get us some logs and fill the hole in as much as we can, to get up under the back tires. Hopefully, that'll give us the boost we need to drive up on out of here."

August smiled. "That's good news."

"Don't get too excited just yet. I'm gonna need your help."

"Tell me what to do and I'll do it."

They foraged the woods for fallen trees and branches that were small enough to drag back to the truck. When they'd stuffed all they could behind the tires, it was time to give it a try.

Caleb asked August to drive and said he would push from the back.

August slowly hung her head. "Umm...I don't know how to drive."

His hands went back to his hips after he'd wiped his muddy hands on his jeans.

"Huh? You never drove before? At *your* age?"

"You say that like I'm an old lady or something!" she snapped.

Caleb wiped his sweaty brow, smearing streaks of mud across his forehead. August expected him to be agitated with her as her father had been, too many times for her to count.

"Sorry. Didn't mean it that way. It's just that kids around here learn how to drive kinda young. I just assumed..."

August cut him off. "Well don't assume anything about me. You don't know the first thing about me."

"You sure are grouchy this morning. Looks like you'll get along with Josie better than I thought. I can see you two are like peas in a pod. On second thought, you just stand over by the trees, far away from the truck and I'll figure it out."

"I didn't say I *wouldn't* help. I just said I didn't know how to drive, and you think it's funny to tease me about it. I'll help. What do you want me to do?"

Caleb shook his head. "Ugh! Girls! You are all enough to drive a sane man crazy! And I mean crazy enough to howl at the moon at midnight! You all sure make it hard for a guy to know what's right to say and what's not. Same with my sister, who is no doubt having a cow about now that I didn't come home last night. She's either mad, worried or both. I gotta get this truck out of here soon or she'll be fit to be tied."

August felt bad for snapping at him. "Tell me what to do, Caleb and I'll do it. Show me how to drive and I'll drive."

Caleb smiled and motioned for her to get into the truck. He turned the motor over and told her to keep her hands on the wheel, put her right foot on the gas and her left foot on the clutch. When he yelled at her to "step on it," she was to push the pedal all the way to the floor until it could go no further. Slowly she was to release her left foot off the clutch. August did as Caleb had shown her to do. After a few minutes of the tires spinning and the entire vehicle rocking forward and back, the truck lurched forward out of the muddy hole. The next thing she knew, she had driven out of the soupy pit. It was the first time she'd ever sat behind the wheel of a moving automobile. Her hands gripped the metal steering wheel with all her might.

Caleb hadn't said anything about what to do once she had driven out of the mud. She heard him yelling in the distance but couldn't make out what he was saying. In the side mirror, she could see him running behind her as he waved his arms wildly in the air.

Caleb ran faster trying to catch up. Finally, August could hear him screaming, "Brake! Step on the brake! Take your foot off the gas!"

Suddenly, she realized that she was still pushing the gas pedal all the way to the floor. She took her foot off the gas and the clutch and put both feet on the brake. The truck came to a crawl before sputtering and jerking back and forth, until it finally stopped.

Caleb caught up to her and told her to move over. She slid into the passenger seat and looked over at him sheepishly to see if he was mad.

He turned toward her with a smile on his face. Dimples on either side of his mouth caught her eye.

"Sorry about that. I was so nervous. I forgot that I still had my foot on the gas."

"That's ok. No harm done. Ya did darn good for your first-time. Although, I thought for a minute you were gonna keep going and leave me right here."

They both laughed as he told her what she looked like behind the wheel as she sped up out of that mud hole and took off like a blaze of glory. In his excitement, he laid his hand on her knee and said, "No big deal. Alls well that ends well, I guess."

His hand on her knee made her flinch. She found it uncomfortable yet welcoming at the same time. He must have noticed her knee jerk response because he withdrew his hand away quickly. There was a longing inside of her to blurt out that it was okay that he had put his hand there, but she didn't. Still, there was a strange longing inside of her to have him put it back.

She'd never felt any sort of physical closeness with another person, but she decided she liked it. Sitting so close to him, she could feel the warmth from his breath, and it felt good to her. She wondered if Caleb had ever been that close to a girl before. If she'd been brave enough, she would have asked him. But she wasn't. Her bravery tank was running low and leaning toward empty. She'd had to tap into it more than she ever imagined she would over the past few days and honestly hoped she wouldn't need to again anytime soon. She hoped she was finally going to be at a place that would be good for her. She prayed that there was someone out there who would be watching over her and see fit that she wound up in a good place with Caleb and his family. A place where she could finally be happy and safe.

Caleb broke the awkward silence. "Well, we best be heading home. I can only imagine what Josie must be thinking about now. Knowing her, she's about to fly off the handle."

"She's probably worried that something bad happened to you."

Caleb smiled. "Doubtful. More like she'll be as angry as a hornet thinking that I met up with some fellas in town or something and forgot to pick you up."

"Why would she think that? You do that often?" August asked, hoping his answer would keep him in the warm, sunny light she saw him in.

Caleb shook his head. "Heck no. There's barely time in a day to do all that needs doing at the farm, let along running around in town. Never enough time in a day it seems."

August cocked her head to the side not understanding. "Well then, why would your sister worry about you running off with some other guys?"

"Trust me, that girl can dream up just about anything and believe it's true. Well...there was that one time and I mean *only* one time; I ran into this guy Tommy, who I used to know from school. I took a few minutes for myself and got into a card game with some guys. We *might* have had a drink or two from Tommy's jug of homemade moonshine. Next thing I knew, I was waking up in a barn, pulling pieces of hay from my mouth with absolutely no idea how I'd gotten there. I decided right then and there that moonshine wasn't going to be for me."

August was stone faced as she listened to him. "And you never drank it again?"

Caleb grinned. "I may be a simple man, but I ain't stupid. Once was enough for me. I didn't care much for not knowing how I ended up in old man Smith's barn. He didn't like it much neither. Told me so as he scurried me out of the place with a shotgun pointed right at me the whole time. Nope. Liquor ain't for me."

August looked toward the window and smiled. She was glad to hear that Caleb didn't want to be a drunk like her father was. She barely knew this boy and it wasn't any of her business, but it made her smile knowing that he wasn't a carbon copy of her father. That is, if Caleb could be trusted and was telling her the truth. Her father had said one thing and done another. This boy could be exactly that kind of person too for all she knew. It was actions she'd be watching out for. It was that simple. Or it should have been. The handsome boy sitting beside her, driving her to his farm, seemed to have some pull on her simply by smiling and revealing his charming dimples. *"How could anyone be untrusting of that face and those dimples?"* August thought to herself.

They drove through the woods on narrow dirt roads that were barely wide enough for the truck. August hoped they didn't meet another vehicle because there was no way the road would be wide enough for two. If Caleb had tried to dodge a single pothole, she'd have not known it. It felt like the entire ride had been one big jostling around in the cab of that farm truck.

"Just up ahead is the farm. Won't be but a minute or two" he announced.

August was grateful for that because her head was pounding from all the tossing around she'd done just to get there.

CHAPTER SIXTEEN

In the distance August could see the outline of a building. As they got closer, she could clearly see the house that Caleb had generously referred to as "the farm." She thought using that word to describe it may have been a stretch of his imagination. It seemed more like a dilapidated shanty that had been taken over by the flock of chickens running wild all over the yard.

To her right a goat was tied to a tree with a rope. Beyond that, a single cow roamed eating grass and flowers from the front yard. August realized that her understanding of farms had only come from the pages of a book, so she was hardly qualified to judge. Still, a shack in the woods with scattered animals running about was never what she had pictured in her mind's eye as a *farm*.

Caleb's eyes widened and a smile spread across his face.

"Well, here it is. Home sweet home! Welcome to our farm."

She could see the pride on his face and asked how long they'd lived there. Not that she really cared to know but she could see that he was proud to talk about it.

"All my life and probably all my father's life was spent here too, but I'm just guessing about that. I don't really know for sure."

A little girl in a yellow and white gingham dress and no shoes on her feet, came running toward Caleb as they got out of the truck. He picked her up and she threw her chubby little arms around his neck.

"August, this here is Grace. She's my baby sister. She doesn't talk but we don't know why...just never has. Even as a little baby, she didn't cry. She still doesn't even cry much now, for some reason."

The child pulled away from Caleb and stared at August trying to size her up. After a few seconds, the little girl smiled.

"I think she likes you." Caleb grinned.

Grace was looking up at August with a wide, toothless smile. She began to tug at August's dress.

"She wants you to pick her up. I'd say you have yourself a new friend." Caleb smiled.

August gently picked up the little girl. She'd never held a child before and was terrified that she might drop her.

"She's so cute." August said as she looked into the tiny little chubby face of Grace. Blonde whisps of her fine hair blew in the wind as the girl continued to stare at August.

About that time, the screen door on the front door flew open with a loud bang and Grace squirmed to get down. She took off running on her short little legs and bare feet in the opposite direction of the house.

"Where in THE HELL have you been? Do you know how much I worried all night? Do you?"

Caleb fidgeted as he shifted from one foot to the other.

"Calm down Josie. It was the truck. Got her stuck just past Dawson's Corner. She was buried deep. We got her out just this morning."

The young girl with her hands on her hips and long blonde hair whipping around with every shake of her head yelled very loudly. Loudly enough so that August felt herself jump a little.

"Calm down? Are you seriously telling me to CALM DOWN? I worried myself sick all night long, thinking something had happened to you, and you come back all smiles and tell me to calm down? You got some nerve Caleb Donnelly!"

Josie stood all of five feet, if that, but August could tell she could more than hold her own.

Caleb once again looked at the ground. "I said I'm sorry..."

"Oh I know what you said. And who is this? This

the girl you picked up at the train station? THIS is what I was sent for help? Good Lord, she looks like a rag tag orphan!"

Some welcome this was turning out to be. She had pinned all her hopes on finally going somewhere decent. Somewhere she could call home, but quickly she could see that this wasn't going to be the case. She'd been through enough in the past few weeks. So much so that somewhere along the way, she'd managed to find her voice. She may have been nothing but a kid with nowhere else to go, but there was no way she was going to stand for anyone trying to make her feel worse than she already did.

"Hey! Wait just a minute. I'm not a "rag-tag" anything, just so ya know."

Josie adjusted her weight from one foot to the other as if to show that she was standing her ground. "Coulda fooled me. From where I'm standing, you look like you just crawled out of a garbage heap."

August scowled, "Now wait just a minute!"

Caleb interrupted them both. "Come on you two. Please stop."

Josie stomped her foot on the wooden planks of the porch. "Do NOT tell me what I can and cannot do around here. As soon as *you* do what I do around here, you can have a say. Until that day, don't even talk to me, Caleb Donnelly!"

She turned and stomped back into the house, slamming the screen door as hard as she could. Caleb looked at August and then quickly at his shoes.

"Sorry about that. Sometimes she gets her

feathers all riled up but she's not really that nasty all the time."

"Well, she can be as nasty as she wants but she better not be throwing it in my direction."

"Come on. Let's go inside and I'll show you around."

"Go in? With that bobtail with its foot caught in a trap? Are you kidding me?"

"Honest, she's harmless. Her bark is way worse than her bite. I promise."

August wasn't sure where this feisty version of herself had come from. She'd never behaved like that before. Of course, that was before she'd met Sal and his sidekick. Everything about her had changed since that day apparently.

"If you say so, Caleb." she muttered as she followed him inside.

From the outside the house hadn't been much to look at. It was in desperate need of a fresh coat of paint and the porch floor needed repair. The boards under her feet felt spongy as she walked over them. Two wooden kitchen chairs sat side by side next to a broken porch swing, that hung sideways from a single chain.

Surprisingly, inside the house was neat and tidy. Caleb opened the door and August followed him inside. A large wooden kitchen table sat in the middle of the room where Josie stood peeling potatoes.

August took a quick look around. "It ain't much but it's home." Caleb said as he waved his hand in the air.

Josie slammed the knife in her hand, onto the wooden table. "Ain't much? Well, it's always been enough to keep us from sleeping in the dirt now hasn't it?"

Once again, August felt bad for Caleb as he hung his head. She was realizing that he did that often around his sister. She imagined that it was a learned behavior from crossing her one too many times. It was quickly becoming apparent to August that Josie was a scrapper and a force to be reckoned with.

"I just meant that...never mind. Welcome to our home, August." He muttered.

"Thank you for letting me stay with you."

She hoped thanking Josie right off the bat may smooth some of the burrs out of her saddle. It had already been a rough enough journey for August, and she didn't need Josie's wrath directed at her.

"By the way, it's *Josephine* to you. My family and people I like call me Josie. That's the *only* people who can. Got it?" she snorted.

She didn't wait for August to answer before she started in on Caleb again.

"Need more wood for the box in the kitchen. If anyone around here thinks they are gonna eat, I need more wood for the stove. Might's well fill up the whole box while you're at it. What's your name, again? Olly?"

"August."

"Strange name. Whatever. April, August, doesn't really matter much to me. You know how to make biscuits?"

August sighed a breath of relief. There wasn't

much she knew about cooking, but thankfully the one thing Rosa had taught her, was how to make biscuits. Finally she could say she knew how to do something. She didn't have to hang her head and say that she had never learned how, like earlier during the driving fiasco. This, she knew.

"Yes, I know how." she declared proudly.

"Good. They ain't going to make themselves. Everything you need will be over there on that shelf."

August looked in the direction toward where Josie nodded and saw the ingredients laid out on a cupboard hutch.

Before she could turn back around, Caleb went outside for more wood leaving her alone with his sister. The tension between them was so thick it could have been cut with a bucksaw. Still, August paid no mind to Josie and set about to making the biscuits just like Rosa had shown her. She thought of the sweet, kind woman as she mixed the flour and baking soda. Her head lost in thought, she didn't notice Josie standing close beside her.

"You just going to stand there stirring that flour while you daydream or you gonna turn it into biscuits?"

August didn't realize she had been daydreaming.

"My mind was somewhere else. I'll throw these together in no time." she smiled.

"I don't know what you're smiling about. Trust me, ain't nothing here to smile about. Are you simple or something? Just get the biscuits in the oven and make it snappy!"

"That's what I'm doing."

"Well not fast enough!" she chided.

August could see that this girl was a younger female version of ole Sal himself. She was going to have to walk softly around there if she intended on staying a single night in the house with Josie. She could see that right away. It was a roof over her head and for that she was grateful. The entire situation may not have been what she pictured in her mind when she set out on the journey to leave Chicago far behind, but it was a place to stay.

Caleb had been a pleasant surprise though. He was a whole lot nicer than his sister. But it wasn't he who "wore the pants" in the family. August thought that life there would be a whole lot nicer if he did.

For the time being, she would do what she was told and would carry her own weight in exchange for a place to lay her head. Secretly though, she would dream of a better life for herself somewhere down the road. She didn't have any choice at the moment. She was only thirteen years old. No money, no family and somewhere in the middle of nowhere. She would work hard and take it from there. She'd suffer through the tantrums that Josephine threw, because she had to.

Much to August's delight, and even to Josie, although she would rather bleed to death biting on her own tongue before she'd ever say so, the biscuits were made in time for dinner and were the best she'd ever made.

Caleb appreciated them too. August saw him

reach for more at least three times.

"August, these biscuits are delicious! Thanks for making them for us." He said as he jammed another half into his mouth.

Josie commented too. "Hmph! I make them all the time, so I don't know what you're over there going on and on about, Caleb Donnelly."

Caleb stopped chewing and had a look on his face that said he knew he'd just put his foot in his mouth. "Yours are great too sis. I was just saying thank you, is all."

"Thank you? Last time I heard those words from you for all I do around here was when?" She didn't wait for him to answer before she began again. "Right! That's what I thought! N-E-V-E-R" she called out, one letter at a time.

Caleb continued to eat and didn't look at her again but that didn't stop Josie from continuing with her rant.

"That's right. Eat up. Both of you because there's plenty of work to do after supper."

Caleb finished eating and headed directly outside without saying a word to anyone.

"Josie, I mean Josephine, I'd be happy to help with the cleanup."

Josie didn't skip a beat before pouring on the sarcasm.

"Really? Well isn't that just sweet of you. Never mind, I can do it. Besides, little Miss who likes to play in mud puddles needs a bath before bed. I assume you can handle *that,* or do I need to do kitchen clean up *and* take care of that too?"

August figured it couldn't be too hard although she certainly had never bathed a child before. "Sure I can do that."

As she stood up to begin filling the metal water buckets that hung behind the wood stove, Josie started in again.

"I should have known that woman would send me someone who didn't know squat and be lazy as all get out. I should have known. You think these dishes are just gonna take themselves from the table to the sink?"

August shook her head. "I thought you wanted me to give the baby a bath?"

"And you think I'm gonna be your maid? Running around and cleaning up after you eat? Think again, Princess."

August quickly realized that there was going to be no way to win with this girl. "Look, I made the biscuits. I'm going to bathe Grace and I'll help with whatever you need after that. I AM here to help you, Josephine."

Josie walked closer to August until she was so close that August felt the warm breath on her face. "Oh, well let me just give you a big ole blue ribbon then."

August shook her head. "I'm trying to show you that I'm grateful for you letting me stay here and I don't want any trouble with you. I really don't."

Josie put her hands on her hips again. "Well then you better stay right off my fightin' side, little girl."

All the hairs on the back of August's neck stood on end. *Little Girl? She's practically the same age as me, for crying out loud.* August was about fed up with people calling her *girl* as though she didn't have a name of her own. She didn't have much, but she did have a name. A name that her Momma had given to her, and she was proud of it for that reason.

"My name's August. I don't like being called GIRL. I have a name of my own."

Josie laughed out loud hysterically. "Oh, really? Well, I think I'll call you whatever I feel like callin' ya. This here's my house and you'd be best off not to forget that."

August took a step forward. "I know it's your house and I said I'm grateful to be here. But the name is AUGUST not GIRL. If you can't deal with that then I'd be just as happy to grab what I came in with and sleep in the barn. Better yet, I'll have Caleb take me back to the train station and you can go back to doing everything on your own."

Josie stepped backward and grinned. "Alright. Alright. I'm sure we can figure this out without you stomping off into the woods or down the road. Kind of soft ain't ya?" She grinned as she turned her back and started pouring dishwater into a basin.

August continued to fill the wash tub with water and enjoyed the silence that had finally overtaken the house. Grace sat at the table playing with a rag doll, oblivious to their bickering.

As if on cue, Caleb came into the house with

an armload of wood as soon as the girls had stopped throwing jabs at one another. "Everything good in here?" he asked.

Josie snapped, "Why wouldn't it be?"

"Just that it sure is quiet in here. Asking if everything's okay, is all." He said as he looked at neither of them but instead looked at little Grace sitting at the table.

Josie spoke first, "Everything's fine. Just mind your own business and get to work."

August saw a smirk creep across Caleb's face. Maybe this arrangement with the Donnelly's would work out okay after all. She highly doubted she and Josie would ever be close or even friends, but hopefully clearing the air right away would make her time there a little more bearable.

After she'd given Grace a bath and got her tucked into bed for the night, August fetched her own tattered bag and grabbed her night dress from it. The bath water was still warm, and she couldn't see wasting it. She closed the curtain to her "room," where she had set up the bath for Grace and slid into the warm water. It felt like heaven as she lowered herself into the tub and let the water cover her bare skin. It had been a long while since she'd been able to have a real bath.

She closed her eyes and thought of Rosa, the single most important person in her life so far. She was grateful for everyone's help along the way, but it was Rosa who had started the chain of events that led her there to that moment. As she laid back against the cool metal tub that looked more like a watering trough than a bathtub, she smiled. Even though she had her doubts about Josie, she was grateful for a place to stay. As she washed away a few days' worth of dust and dirt, the warm water felt like heaven against her skin.

She quickly opened her eyes when she heard the rings of the curtain slide against the rod.

"Oh my. Oh my goodness. I'm so sorry!" he stammered.

It was Caleb. He stood frozen in place as though unable to move. His hands covered his eyes as he apologized repeatedly.

"August, I'm so sorry. I didn't know you were in the bath. I'm so sorry. I was just..."

August quickly covered her chest, not that she had much to cover she realized. She saw that Caleb's face had turned a shade or two of red that she'd never seen on anyone's face before. The quivering of his voice sounded like he was about to start crying.

"It's okay, Caleb. Just go. Keep your eyes covered and go. Close that curtain behind you please."

"Yes ma'am. I'm sorry."

August could see that he was truly embarrassed at having walked in on her while she was naked in the bath. *She* was embarrassed too. Josie was not much older than her and had seemed to develop a whole lot faster than she had. She felt suddenly aware of that as she looked down at her own body. She looked more like a flat chested child rather than a young woman like Josie had grown into. August had no idea why that fact had suddenly made her feel uncomfortable. Her body was something she'd never thought about in that way before.

As she dressed and walked into the kitchen, Caleb was standing at the sink with his back to her. He had a metal dipper of water in his hand and was just standing there staring out the window as he slowly sipped.

Her face began to feel flush just seeing him there, gazing out the window. Was he thinking about what he'd just seen? What did he think about what he'd seen? She felt a need for air and couldn't get to the front door fast enough. She ran down the steps and continued up the road she'd come down hours earlier. With no idea where she was running to, she ran. When she could run no more, she stopped and dropped her head to her knees as she tried to catch her breath. Her heart beating in time with the pulsing in her ears.

Why had she felt the need to run out of the house like that? Where did she think she was going to go? Even if she wanted to leave, she had no idea where she'd go. She felt lightheaded. She didn't know what was going on with her, but she knew it had something to do with Caleb.

After she'd stopped long enough to catch her breath, she started back toward the house. It was almost dark, and she was exhausted.

Caleb was sitting on the front steps fiddling with a piece of wood and a knife. He looked up when he saw her and immediately went back to shaving slivers. Even when she'd reached the steps, he didn't look up.

"Sometimes, a body just needs to run. Fast. Like the wind kind of fast. Helps to clear away the cobwebs."

August smiled. "You're right about that. I feel tired now but better. Goodnight Caleb."

"Goodnight Ms. August."

August was grateful that they didn't discuss him walking in on her in the bath. The fact that he'd seen her naked was embarrassing enough.

Once in her room, behind the curtain, which was usually Caleb's room, she smiled at the number of books on the desk by the window. She wouldn't have taken him for a boy that liked to read. Most of the titles pertained to woodworking or forestry, and she smiled to see that reading was also something he obviously cared about.

She decided she liked him. So far. She would need to get to know him a whole lot more before she could really decide how much. His sister, now that was another story. August knew that any drop of kindness from that girl was going to have to be earned a hundred times over and maybe not even then.

Baby Grace was a bit of a mystery. It seemed to August that since the girl was old enough to walk, she should be talking or at least babbling. But she wasn't. August had been there most of the day and not once had she heard the child utter a single sound. It seemed like Grace was a person trapped inside a tiny little body. She wondered what had happened to make the child unable to speak or at least make some sort of sound. Caleb hadn't really gone into the reasons. One day when they were out of earshot of his sister, August would ask more about that.

Time would tell how she'd make out at the Donnelly farm. For the moment, she was exhausted. Sleep was all she wanted.

CHAPTER SEVENTEEN

The loud clattering of pots and pans in the kitchen woke August even before she heard the rooster crow. Morning seemed to have come quick. Too quick. She figured Josie must be cooking and she knew she wouldn't hear the end of it if she had to do it all alone. August quickly dressed into the only outfit she had that wasn't so dirty it could stand up on its own. As she dressed, she heard an axe slicing through dry wood outside her window. Caleb was already up too. She was the last one to be up and at it. There was no way she wouldn't be goaded by Josie for that.

August had a feeling that Josie looked for things to complain about and without meaning to, she had given her ammunition to use against her.

She took a deep breath and walked into the kitchen. Sure enough, Josie had been waiting to hear her footsteps hit the floor so she could begin the day's guilt trip. Her back was to August, and she kept it that way. Although seeing Josie's face wasn't necessary to know there was a big sarcastic smirk on it.

"So nice of you to grace us with your presence today. Is there anything I can get for you? A six-course gourmet meal perhaps? Or maybe you'd rather climb back into bed and have your morning meal *brought* to you?"

August knew it was coming but that didn't make it any less annoying. What time was it anyway? She couldn't have slept *that* long, could she?

"What time is it?" she asked.

"Time? You want to know the time? Do you have somewhere you need to be today, Princess?"

"No. Josephine, I don't. I was just wondering how long I slept."

Josie laughed. "I'd say you slept quite well since you slept half the day away already."

"Really? Half the day?"

"Yes Ma'am. It's almost six a.m., Caleb and I have been up for hours already. Working, as you can see."

August rolled her eyes and stifled a chuckle, but not deep enough because Josie heard it.

"Something funny?" she asked as she spun around on her heels to face August. Her face was red though August didn't know yet if it was from anger or standing over the hot stove.

"Nothing is funny. I just don't think that six

a.m. is sleeping half the day away."

"Once again, what you think hardly matters to me whatsoever. And around here, six is late. We get to bed early and up at daybreak. That's when the work starts. You best remember that going forward."

She turned back to the cookstove and continued stirring whatever it was that she was making.

"Go outside. Caleb will show you how to do barn chores today. Tomorrow you'll be on your own. He can't be taking time away from his own work to help you every day, so you better be a quick learner."

August didn't bother to respond and was glad to get out of the house. Whatever she had to do for outside chores, she'd gladly welcome them. At least she'd be away from Josie's judgmental eyes.

She found Caleb at the woodpile leaning on an axe with one hand and grabbing a piece of split wood with the other. He looked up when he saw her.

"Morning, August. I hope you slept well." He brushed the sweat from his forehead with the back of his hand.

"Morning. I slept well. Too well, according to your sister, who says that I have wasted half the day already."

Caleb laughed. "Oh, don't listen to her. Pay no mind to her sour disposition. When she gets used to you being around, I'm sure she'll be a little more friendly."

August raised her eyebrows. "I don't know about that. I have a tough time believing she's *ever* nice. To anyone."

Caleb conceded. "Okay. You may be right about that more than you know. I should have said I *hope* she'll come around."

August smiled. "Yeah, me too. She said I am to learn how to do chores with you today."

Caleb smiled from ear to ear revealing his dimples. "Sure thing. Grab some of these chunks of wood and help me stack them will you?"

When the split wood had been stacked, Caleb brought her up the path that ran alongside the house. "Barns just up here over that hill. That's where all the animals are. For the most part anyway. Once in a while one of 'em runs off and makes its way to the front yard."

"Oh, I thought you just had the one cow and the little goat I saw tied to a tree yesterday."

Caleb laughed at the thought. "That's funny. Nope. We have cows, pigs, goats, and chickens."

August realized that her first impression of their "pitiful" farm had been completely wrong. As they came to the top of the hill, she was surprised to see endless green fields and a big red barn sitting smack dab in the middle of it all. She felt bad for thinking that Caleb had been exaggerating about his farm. What she was looking at was a far cry from a runaway goat, one cow, and some rogue chickens.

"Wow! This is all yours?" she asked.

"Well, it's the family farm. It's not as big as it used to be but with just me here to run it, it's plenty big enough."

Inside the barn there were stalls for cows, a pen

for goats, and more chickens scurrying around. In the back of the barn, was a pig pen. All of them were apparently waiting for Caleb because they all began to squeal non-stop when they saw him.

"Sounds like they like you." August teased.

"They like the food they get from me. I don't think they much care who gives it to them."

August wasn't sure she believed that. Caleb filled a bucket with grain and quickly had an audience of goats milling around him. He took the time to pat the top of each one's head and call them by name, before getting into the pen.

"You know all their names? How can you remember what name belongs to what goat? They all look so much alike." she giggled.

He smiled. "Stick around, and you'll learn who they all are too. Each one of 'em has their own personality. You'll see."

After the goats were fed and their pens cleaned, she put fresh hay on the floor, and Caleb showed her how to do the same for the cow stalls.

"We clean the cow stalls while they are outside. Makes it much easier. After each one is clean, we put hay down and grain in the bin. Then I have them come in and I milk while they eat. Here I'll call one in and show you what I mean."

August smiled and wondered how he planned to "call" a cow into the barn. Somehow she doubted that yelling out a name, to a cow, would make it come running as a dog would. Then again, for all she knew about animals, they could behave the same as a dog.

This was her first experience on a farm and her first contact with any kind of animal.

She knew her skills were limited, at best, on most things, but she was enjoying learning how to do new things. In the brief time on her journey, she'd learned so much already. Things she never imagined learning. Like how to hide in the dark and slow her breathing down so as not to be heard by anyone who may be close by. And how to bake biscuits and how to throw together a stew from whatever ingredients are on hand. She'd be forever grateful to Rosa for teaching her those things.

And now she was learning to take care of farm animals. Also something she'd never dreamed of doing. To some it may be seen as a tiresome chore; something to be dreaded. To August it was a lot more enjoyable to shovel manure than to be locked in a room with children with shaved heads and no clothes to wear. She was also perfectly aware of the fact that she could be dressed in barely anything, serving drinks to drunken men, drooling all over her.

She smiled as she followed Caleb and cleared her mind of the unhappy thoughts of Sal and what her life could have been. She laughed out loud for the first time in ages, watching firsthand as Caleb had indeed called in the first cow for milking. He didn't call them cows. He called them his "girls." One by one, he called them in by name. He started with "Bossy Mama." He lured her in with a song that went like this:

"Oh once there was a Bossy Mama, she loved ole Caleb more than grass and if she didn't come a running when he called; she feared he'd kick her in the as…she comes a running he grabs up her favorite feed."

August leaned against the open barn door in disbelief as Bossy Mama and *only* Bossy Mama came trotting into a stall where Caleb stood.

"You have got to be kidding me!" she laughed so hard that her stomach hurt.

Caleb smiled. "What? You thought she wasn't going to like my singing?"

When she caught her breath again she answered him. "I have never, ever heard of a cow that comes running into a barn for a song! That's so silly."

Caleb was still smiling as he patted Bossy Mama's back before he began to milk her. "You hear that, girl? August here thinks we're silly."

She was still laughing. "I didn't mean that in a bad way. I mean silly but neat. Unusual but neat. Yeah, that's what I meant to say."

Caleb looked at her with that smile that made her face warm. "So you've seen a lot of cows come in from the pasture, have you?"

He was teasing her, and she was starting to figure him out enough to see that now. She didn't mind teasing when it came from him. Seems all he had to do was smile and she found herself smiling back without meaning to.

Every now and again as she shoveled out the stalls, she would look over at Caleb and smile. It didn't matter what cow he wanted to come in, the song worked on every one of them. One by one until he'd done all the milking, he had lured them in with that silly song.

When he was finished, he came to her at the far end of the barn. "Having fun?"

August nodded her head. "I don't mind it at all."

Caleb could see that she was enjoying herself. She was some sort of different girl than he'd ever known before.

"You wouldn't rather be inside cooking or sewing or something like that?" he asked.

August laughed loudly. "Inside cooking with your sister breathing down my neck and shooting insults at me all day? Nope. I think I get along better with the animals."

He laughed like he thought she was kidding but she wasn't joking about that. Not at all. When they had finished with the goats, pigs, and cows, she was introduced to the chicken coop.

"C'mon I'll show you how to handle a coop full of chickens. They need to go outside so we can muck out the coop. Also, we need to gather the eggs from under the hens, so we need them outside. I'll warn you ahead of time, it's rancid smelling in there during the summer."

The thought of Sal popped into her mind again. "That's okay. I can do it. Stinky or not, there's worse things I could be doing, I'm sure."

"Remember that when one of the hens bites you." he teased.

August's eyes widened, "Bite? Chickens bite?"

"Not really bite, but they may peck at ya to keep

ya away from their eggs is all."

As soon as he opened the door to the coop, August realized that Caleb hadn't been joking about the stench inside. The smell was so strong, her eyes began to water. He heard her gasp and hold her breath.

"Knocks the wind right out of ya at first, don't it?" he said as he saw her plug her nose. "Give it a minute. When the fresh air gets in through the door, it'll go away a little bit. Either that or you just get used to it." he grinned.

"Not sure that's something I want to learn to like."

"Oh you don't got to like it; just get used to it a little bit, so it won't knock ya backward soon as ya open up the door."

August nodded but knew that there was no way she was ever going to "get used" to that stench.

"Truth is, it shouldn't be this bad in here. It is right now because there's only me that's been working around here. By the time I finish with the other animals and the barn chores, I haven't had the time to put in over here at the coop. I was hoping you might do the chicken chores a few times a week, so it don't get this bad?"

August nodded, "I'll clean it out every single day."

"That sure would be a big help to me, August. There's a whole load of chickens around here that's going to love ya for that."

He showed her how to collect eggs from underneath a hen and before she knew it, they had an entire basket full.

"Ya done really good with the chores. I'll make a farmer out of you yet." He grinned.

It felt good to hear that she had done a respectable job at something. She'd gone most of her life not knowing the pride in a job well done. And for some reason, that she didn't yet understand, she liked the feeling of pleasing Caleb. There was something about that boy that made her want to draw kind words out of him. Even if it was for a job well done shoveling manure.

CHAPTER EIGHTEEN

For the next few weeks, August continued to do barn chores alongside Caleb. Always, when she finished, she'd go inside and ask Josie if there was something she could do to help her. The response was always the same. "No. Don't bother now. I've already done it all myself." Or something as equally dismissive.

It was part of her personality August learned. The longer she stayed with them at the farm, the more she realized that Josie simply enjoyed being miserable. Nothing anyone could say to her was going to change that.

If it was sunny outside, it was too hot for Josie. If it rained, it was too wet. If the rooster crowed before she opened her eyes, that ruined her day. August understood that it was always going to be that way with Josie.

Caleb had more free time now that he was getting help with the farm chores. Every afternoon that the sun was shining, he would take August down to the pond and teach her how to fish. Once she'd gotten the hang of it, they had a competition to see who could catch the most fish. The rules were that only trout were counted; all others they tossed back into the pond.

Caleb was ahead in the count, but August didn't care. She didn't care if she ever caught a single fish. She was simply happy to be out there spending time with him. Spending time with a boy and in nature, was something she never realized could be so fun. Watching fields, rivers, and forest from a moving car was nothing like feeling the ground on her bare feet. She'd sit for hours at the edge of the water, dipping her toes into the cool pond and watching the clouds pass over.

Every now and again, Caleb would look her way and grin. "What are you smiling about over there?"

She'd return the smile. "Oh, nothing much. Just waiting for that school of trout to swim by so I can catch every last one of 'em."

Caleb would laugh and they'd go back to being quiet again. August enjoyed feeling the sun on her skin and the cool breeze that swept through the tall grasses around the pond. The smell of wildflowers and the scent from the pine trees filled her with peace.

Something she'd never understood before. The peace of being content.

She also enjoyed simply spending time with Caleb. He didn't act like he wished she weren't there. He never made her feel like being with her was the absolute worst punishment. The feeling of acceptance by someone was something completely new to August and she liked it. She enjoyed how something as simple as smiling made her feel. Until she met Caleb, she never felt like there was much to smile about.

August noticed how she smiled much of the time now. Even in the face of the resentment she received from Josie, she found herself smiling back at her. She was beginning to understand that her own happiness was what mattered. Her body and soul felt good when she smiled at Josie instead of lashing out like she wanted to.

That day, she caught two fish and Caleb proudly boasted the four he'd taken from the pond. As they got ready to head back for supper, August walked fast to keep up with Caleb. His long legs gave him a much bigger stride than her own.

"I'd say someone is getting good at this fishing thing. Ya caught almost as many as I did today."

August smiled. "Look out tomorrow. It just might be the day I kick your butt at this *fishing thing*." she teased.

Caleb's laughter filled the forest and August couldn't help but smile. Out of the corner of her eye, she saw his head tilt back as he laughed. She'd never met anyone quite like him. There was a kindness about him that she didn't know could come from a male. She felt comfortable and safe with him, which was something she thought she'd never feel again.

Walking into the yard, a wave of panic swept over August. A car she didn't recognize was in the yard. No one was in it which meant whoever the vehicle belonged to, was inside the house.

She heard her voice crack as she asked Caleb if he knew who the car belonged to.

"That car? Oh, that's just Deacon Berry. He comes around every now and again to get biscuits and other baked goods from Josie. Since the depression hit, flour has been hard for folks to come by. We stocked up as much as the cellar would hold, so we still have plenty. The church orders goods from Josie for their suppers and special events. It's a good deal for us too because it brings in a little extra money."

August stood completely still. "You're sure that's who it is?" her heart pounding and her hands shook as she waited for an answer.

Caleb looked at her. "Of course I'm sure. Hey you okay? You look like you've seen a ghost."

August took a deep breath and put her hands on her knees, trying to catch her breath. "Yeah, I'm alright."

Caleb was looking at her strangely. "What was that about?"

She shook her head. "I don't know, maybe I'm just hungry or tired. I'm okay."

Caleb put his hand on her shoulder. "That

looked more like you were scared half to death. Are you afraid of something? Or someone?"

August shook her head. "No. It's nothing, really. I'm okay. Let's go in for supper."

"Okay, but if there's anything you ever want to talk about, I'm a good listener. At least that's what Bossy Mama and her friends think."

They both laughed as they walked into the house. August was relieved that he didn't press her more even though she knew it was obvious to him that she was scared of something, or someone. But she was glad he let it go. Caleb may not had much of an education, but he was people smart. He could see that she was terrified and bright enough to know she wasn't ready to talk about whatever it was that had made her act that way. August doubted she'd ever be ready to talk to Caleb about what had happened back in Chicago. It wasn't something she wanted to share with *anyone*.

All Josie and Caleb knew was that she needed a place to stay and fortunately, had never asked her why. August was sure they must have wondered why a thirteen-year-old girl was on her own in the world. She was grateful that they were the type of people to mind their own business.

As they opened the front door, Deacon Berry was just leaving. His deep-set, dark eyes looked right through August and a cold chill ran through her entire body. He never took his eyes off her even though he was speaking to Caleb. She had a bad feeling about that man. His crooked smile and beady eyes told her more about the person wearing the fancy suit than any words ever could have.

Suddenly she felt goosebumps rise on her skin and pop up all over her body. She felt just like she did when she saw Sal sitting at his desk smiling at her in a way that made her feel dirtier than she'd ever felt before. There was something about Deacon Berry that she didn't care for even if she couldn't put her finger on the reason why yet. Caleb may think the good Deacon was a stand-up respectable member of the community, but August's gut was telling her a different story.

"Hello, Miss. I don't believe we've met. My name is Deacon Berry. Pleasure to meet you." He extended his hand for her to shake but she was not touching that man.

She offered a half smile. "Pleasure" was all she said.

She felt Caleb's gaze turn toward her when she offered the Deacon no further conversation or her hand. She'd talk to him about it later if she had to, but for the moment, she felt like she wanted the floor to open right there and swallow her whole. August had the feeling that Deacon Berry knew she had him pegged even though they'd just met. He tipped his hat and said goodbye to them.

Josie quickly turned her back to them as they came into the kitchen. August noted a look of discomfort on her flushed face. She wasn't quite sure what that was all about but somehow felt it had to do with the snake oil salesman, disguised as a Deacon.

She didn't trust that man as far as she could throw him. Maybe Josie felt the same? August wished she were closer to her so she could ask. But they didn't have that kind of friendship. They didn't have a friendship at all. The only words they shared had to do with chores.

She was allowing August to stay there and help on the farm, but she never went out of her way to make her feel comfortable. At that moment, the look on Josie's face sure looked a whole lot like shame to August. *Had the Deacon done something to her while he was alone in the house with her?* she wondered. She hoped not because she knew in her heart that Caleb would lose his mind if that were the case.

"You two get any fish for supper or have you just been fiddling around all afternoon while I worked my fingers to the bone?" she grumbled.

Caleb spoke first. "We've got fish for dinner sis. We both caught our share today. August here is turning into quite the little fisherman. Or should I say fisherwoman?" He laughed.

Josie turned her head around like it was on a swivel, "Oh please, give me a break. You threw a line in the water and a fish came along and bit it. Real hard work that musta been. And she is not a *woman*. She's just a dumb kid."

"Geeze, Josie. Why ya always got to be so mean?" he asked.

"It's not mean ya Dumb Dumb! It's the truth. That's a word I'm sure neither of you have heard before. Maybe when you get older, you'll understand what I'm talking about."

Caleb laughed. "You do know that you're not much older than us, right?"

Josie stood in the middle of the kitchen in her usual staunch manner with both hands on her hips. "Oh really? I guess you don't know that hard work ages a person far beyond their years. In that case, this makes me twice the age of both of you dimwits. Now quit being mouthy and go outside and clean those fish if you plan on eating them tonight."

August felt her eyebrows raise. That girl was so dramatic, she almost couldn't stand it. She knew Josie worked hard. They all worked hard. Acting like she was the only one who ever did anything was really starting to get on her nerves..

Once outside, she asked Caleb, "Has she always been like that? Acting like she's the only one who does anything?"

"If that's a real nice way to ask if she's always been such a pain in the butt, then the answer is yes. Drives me straight up a wall some days."

August agreed. "Good. I'm glad it's not just me."

"You? Why, you don't drive me up a wall at all Ms. August." he grinned.

"Oh no. I didn't mean…Never mind. Hey, what about that Deacon guy?"

Caleb shrugged. "What about him?"

She watched while he cleaned the fish and thought of how to tell Caleb that she didn't trust the Deacon.

"I don't know. He gave me the willies."

Caleb laughed. "What? Deacon Berry? He's a good man. He's one of those goody two shoes from town. Likes his religion a bit too much for me but wouldn't hurt a flea."

"So you say. I say there's something not right about that man. You notice how your sister seemed all out of sorts when we came into the house?"

"When *isn't* she out of sorts?" he joked. "Here, grab one of these trout and help me so we can get them on the stove. I'm starving and I still have the cows to feed after dinner."

August picked up a trout and began to clean it like he'd shown her. All the while she was thinking about Deacon Berry and Sal. In her mind, she saw a real thin line separating the two. One a heathen criminal. The other a religious criminal. Or at least that was the judgement she'd made in her own mind. Other people, like Caleb and Josie could believe whatever they wanted about the "upstanding" Deacon, but her gut told her all she needed to know.

CHAPTER NINETEEN

Early the next week, Josie and August miraculously managed to work alongside one another in the kitchen. Josie had a big order going to the church for coffee and tea cakes as well as bread for an upcoming Communion. Given that the amount of baking was larger than usual, Josie didn't seem to mind that she had someone in her kitchen.

August was glad and a bit surprised at the lighter side of Josie's personality as they worked. She almost dropped a ceramic bowl when she heard Josie humming a song. She wasn't sure what had gotten into her or what had made her *that* happy, but August wished she saw that side of her more often.

Not once in the hours of cooking together was

August scolded for not doing something right. It seemed that everything she did was perfectly fine with Josie. Something was going on; August just didn't know exactly what it was yet.

One time, she'd even heard laughter come from her. "You seem so happy today."

Josie smiled. "Do I? Oh, same as every other day, I suppose."

August almost choked. Who was she kidding? If only Josie *was* like this every day, but she wasn't. Not even close.

She chose her words carefully because she liked the lighter side of Josie and didn't want to say something to set her off. The last thing August wanted was to hear the humming stop and the yelling start.

"Well, it's just that today you seem *extra* happy. That's what I meant to say."

Josie smiled. "Thank you" was all she said.

Later when Deacon Berry knocked at the door, August noticed the redness flow into Josie's cheeks. Just as they had the last time he'd visited.

"August, why don't you take Grace and go help Caleb in the barn?"

She was trying to get rid of them and August could see it. "Oh there's no way we could do that. Not with all that you have going on here in the kitchen. I'll stay and help you load all the baking into the truck. Not to mention all the cleanup there is to do. I couldn't have you do all of that alone."

"I won't be by myself, Marcus is…I mean, Deacon Berry will help me. You two run along now and give

Caleb a hand" she said, dismissing them both.

August thought her breakfast was about to find its way from her stomach and land straight onto the floor. She *wanted* to be alone with that man? That man who was old enough to be her father and gave August the willies? August took Grace by the hand and led her to the barn. She knew there was something creepy about that man and Josie's disgusting excitement to be alone with him confirmed to her that something bad was going on. Something very, very bad.

A grown man doing God knows what with a young girl not much older than August herself? How had Caleb not seen this for himself? No matter, August knew what was going on inside the house and she felt sick thinking about it. There would be no way any man, especially an old man like the Deacon, would be putting his hands on her.

"Caleb, you ever notice how your sister acts when that Deacon guy comes around?"

He was busy milking the cows and shook his head.

"I don't know what you mean."

"Really? You never noticed how giddy and flushed in the face she gets when he comes around?"

He shook his head again. "Nah, can't say I have. Besides, it's usually milking time when he drops in."

August rolled her eyes. "How convenient." she thought.

"But if she's happy, it's probably because she likes the extra cash he pays her for the baking."

August looked up at the roof of the barn in total disbelief at how unaware and innocent Caleb could be.

THE ROAD TO MARIETTA

"Yeah, I'm sure that's it. It's her *baking* he comes all the way out here for."

"What's that? I didn't hear what you said."

There was no use continuing the conversation with Caleb. He was oblivious to anything going on with his sister and Deacon Berry.

"Oh, nothing. I was just agreeing with you is all."

Grace was tugging at her dress trying to tell her that she'd stepped in a cow patty but by the time August understood what she was trying to say, she had completely fallen bottom first into a large pile of manure. The poor child was covered from head to toe and wailing at the top of her lungs.

"What's wrong with Grace? I can't believe she's actually crying and loudly at that!" Caleb yelled over the blatting from his baby sister.

"She's okay. She fell into a pile of manure and isn't liking it by the sounds. I'll take her up to the house and get her cleaned up."

"Thanks, August. Hey, when you're done, do you think you can give me a hand with the milking? I'm only about halfway through and at this rate, it'll be morning before I'm done."

"Sure. I'll come back after I get Grace cleaned up. I'll be back."

All the way to the house, Grace sounded as though she'd broken a bone or something worse. "It's ok Grace. It'll wash right off. Now hush, you'll be all clean again in no time."

Opening the door, August was surprised to see no one around. She walked to the stove and poured a pitcher of warm water into the wash bin. She took the dirty clothes off Grace and got her cleaned up. Strangely, she still hadn't seen hide nor hair of Deacon Berry or Josie. When August climbed the stairs to get a clean outfit for the little girl, she heard muffled voices. Voices that sounded winded, like they were gasping for air. She slowly pushed open the door to Josie's bedroom, where Grace's clothes were kept. When the door opened, she saw Deacon Berry on top of Josie and neither of them had any clothes on.

August froze. She tried to look away and ordered her feet to move but they felt like they were stuck in hardened cement. She wanted to back out of the room quietly and forget that she had ever been there. That plan went right out the window when she heard a voice that she realized was her own, yell out, "Oh My God! Oh My God!"

Deacon Berry jumped off the bed like he was on fire. He grabbed his trousers and threw them on in seconds flat. Josie covered herself with the blanket from the bed but made no motion to get up. The Deacon flew down the stairs two at a time and ran out the front door like he had a nest full of red ants in his underwear.

Josie started yelling, "What in THE Hell do you think you're doing in here? This is MY room!"

"I came up to get a clean outfit for Grace. But I think the real question here should be what are YOU doing?"

"That's none of your business. You tell another living soul about this, and I'll make sure you'll be sorry! THAT is all you need to know. You hear me?"

August was still stuck in place. "I think I'm going to be sick."

"I mean it! Caleb doesn't hear about this, and I mean EVER. You cross me and you'll regret it! Don't push me, girl."

August raised her brow. "Don't worry. Your dirty little secret is safe with me but only because the last thing I want to do is to hurt your brother. He'd go after that greaseball and end up in the hoosegow for the rest of his life. Not that *you* would care about that, but I would."

"You make sure it stays that way. I mean it. Or you WILL be sorry."

August ignored the threat, grabbed a clean outfit for the baby, and left the room. After Grace was ready for bed, she rocked her in the chair until she was out for the night. She yelled upstairs to let Josie know she was going out to help Caleb finish the milking.

"Don't you dare tell him!" she screamed.

August dismissed the tirade. "Yeah. Yeah. I heard you the first ten times, Josie. Nobody wants to know your disgusting secret, trust me."

CHAPTER TWENTY

August was confused and nauseous when she walked outside. The Deacon's car was parked in the yard, but he was nowhere to be seen. She hadn't noticed if the cakes and breads were still on the kitchen table or not. But if they weren't gone from the table and loaded in his car, they should have been. For that matter, he should have been in the car too and gone down the road toward home by that time. But he wasn't. So where was he?

Dusk was settling in, making it difficult to see too far ahead of her. What she *could* clearly see was that the "good" Deacon wasn't anywhere in sight. She didn't understand where he could have gone. He'd run out of the house earlier like a man on fire. She figured he was running for his car in shame after what she'd walked in on. He should have been.

August stood at the bottom of the steps and slowly turned in circles trying to catch a glimpse of any movement. A barn owl flew down from a high branch of a tree and sent her heart racing, but it was the only thing moving in the evening air. Had he been crazy enough to see Caleb in the barn? She decided that wasn't where he had gone. She had a sneaking suspicion that he was too much of a coward to face up to what he'd done. Facing Josie's brother after he'd just been caught in his sister's bedroom, would be or should be, the *last* place he'd want to be.

She approached the car and noticed that the baked goods she and Josie had made were loaded in the back seat of the car. He had taken the time to load the car, but he hadn't left. Why? What was that underhanded creep up to? She certainly planned to ask him just as soon as she could find him.

The lights in the barn were still lit, and she knew that Caleb had a few hours left to work before the chores would be done. She would go back to the barn as she'd agreed to do. Hopefully, the Deacon hadn't made the grave mistake of going to see Caleb. August feared what she might find at the barn if he had.

She grabbed a lantern from the front porch and set out for the barn. On the way, she thought of what she would say to Caleb. She knew that she'd have to carefully choose her words. If she didn't, she could make the entire situation so much worse than it already was. She'd come to care for Caleb in the short time she'd been staying at the farm. Hurting him was something she didn't want to do. Now the wormy Deacon, on the other hand, was a whole different story. There were a million things running through her head that she'd like to do to that man. All of them would land her in prison.

If she'd been an adult and a much stronger person, she'd love to teach that man a lesson or two. Though she knew *she* couldn't do it, she sure wished that he would come up against someone bigger and stronger than himself to teach him that lesson. As much as she wanted to see that, she didn't want Caleb to be the one to do it.

If he were to lay a hand on that man, and he certainly would, if he knew what August had walked in on, he would ruin his entire life. It would kill him to have to leave his sisters on their own. They wouldn't be able to stay together if something happened to bring attention to the fact that they were all minor children living on their own without adult guardians. All their lives there at the farm would surely be ruined and that was the last thing she wanted for any of them. Even Josie.

August knew that she would be best off to forget that anything had happened. If only she could. She'd have to think carefully before opening her mouth to Caleb. He was expecting her to help with the chores and that's what she was going to do. Period. Hopefully, by the time the barn chores were finished, they would return to the house and find the Deacon's car gone. Otherwise, things were apt to get messy. Very messy.

As she climbed the hill, August's heart skipped a beat or two when she heard the snapping of twigs somewhere in the darkness around her. She hadn't been outside after dark alone before now and quickly remembered why. She hated the dark. There were things roaming at night that she couldn't see. But they could see her. She could feel eyes on her even though she couldn't see what they belonged to. It was an unnerving feeling to know she had the disadvantage of not being able to see in the dark. Her hands shook as she held the lantern higher trying to light up as much of the woods as she could.

In the distance, she was relieved to see the shadows of the barn lights illuminating the spaces between the trees. Still, she was getting more nervous with every step because she noticed that the snapping of branches stopped when she stopped walking. Whatever she was sharing the woods with, was copying her exact movements.

"C'mon August. Put one foot in front of the other and make a run for the barn. Quit being a baby." She told herself.

She had only taken a step forward with her eyes glued straight ahead for the barn when she felt a hard shove forward. She dropped the lantern as her body hit the ground with a hard thud. Everything went dark.

She had no idea how long she'd been out. As she began to slowly open her eyes, she could feel the heavy pounding in her head. A warm sensation trickled down the back of her neck. Trying to clear the fog from her eyes, she saw the outline of a person standing above her.

"Caleb?" she whispered.

A deep voice answered, "I bet you wish I were don't you? You naughty lil thing."

August felt her body tremble as she lay defenseless on the ground. "Deacon? Deacon Berry?"

She pushed herself up onto her elbows, trying to understand where she was and what had happened. A heavy thump to the side of her head sent her back to the ground with force. Her world went dark once again.

CHAPTER TWENTY-ONE

"August wake up!"

It was Caleb's voice, but she couldn't see him. She couldn't see anything. Her head felt like a two-ton brick had hit her. Even her eyes were in pain. Everything hurt. She felt like a hot, sharp knife was piercing through both of her eyes.

"August, it's me, Caleb. Listen, Ya gotta wake up. We gotta get out of here!"

"What happened to..."

"No time for that now. I'll explain later. Right now, the woods are on fire, and we've gotta get back to the farm and quick."

August tried to understand. "What? Fire? Where is..."

"I'm going to pick ya up and carry ya over my shoulder, August. When I do, ya hold on tight. I'm going to have to move fast, and I don't want to drop ya. Can you hear me?"

It took every bit of strength she had to nod to show that she understood. August tried to help lift her body, but it was no use. Her entire body was numb and had become dead weight. The night air suddenly felt cold and damp against her skin. How long had she been unconscious? How long had she laid there on the ground? What hit her beside the head to land her on the ground in the first place? Every thought she had was jumbled together, and she wasn't able to separate a single one. As Caleb walked with her over his shoulder, her jostling body made the painful throbbing in her skull stronger with each step he took.

Once at the house, Caleb gently laid her on her bed. "I've got to go back and try to contain the fire before it reaches the house or the barn. Rest until I get back, okay?"

August was so confused. "Fire? What fire? Caleb, what's going on?"

He didn't have time to explain. "Tell you all about it just as soon as I can."

She felt like she'd been hit over the head with a giant hammer. She must have tripped in the dark and hit her head on a rock or something equally as hard. The last thing she remembered was the warm, cozy feeling of the bed.

Sometime later, though she had no idea how much later, August opened her eyes again. She knew she was in her bed but had no recollection of how she'd gotten there.

"You've decided to come back to us, I see." It was Josie at her bedside.

"Huh? What do you mean?"

"You've been somewhere else for a couple of days now."

"I have? Where have I been?"

"How in tarnation would I know? You hit your head quite hard the other night, I'd guess. Almost burned the whole farm down too."

August had no idea what Josie was talking about. "Fire? There was a fire?"

"Oh, there most certainly was. Good thing Caleb was able to stop it too. Otherwise, you would have taken every last thing we own from us."

August opened her eyes wide as she started to remember Caleb throwing her over his shoulder and carrying her back to the farm. "I think I remember. A fire..."

"I'm not sure how you *wouldn't* remember. You dropped the lantern and nearly destroyed this whole place." Her voice filled with sarcasm and obvious blame.

All at once, the events of that night started to come back to August. Her body shook uncontrollably. "I remember that. I remember that night. Yes, I do remember. I was smacked on the head, with something. I must have dropped the light."

Josie laughed. "Hit on the head? That's funny. I do believe you are absolutely off your rocker."

"No, I'm not. I'm telling you I was HIT over my head. Well, not at first. First, I was pushed and hit my head on the ground but after that I was hit. Right here on the side of my head." She touched the side of her head and winced at the large tender lump that had formed.

Josie was listening to her with wide eyes disbelieving everything August said. "That's quite a story. Did the boogeyman come out of the woods and knock you out?"

August was scared and shaking as she started to remember piece by piece. "No. It wasn't any boogeyman it was your good friend, that Deacon man."

Josie howled with laughter. "Deacon Berry? You're saying that Deacon Berry hid out in the woods waiting for you? Then what? He hit you in the head and started the forest on fire?"

August scooted herself up in the bed. "I'm telling you the truth. You've got to believe me, Josephine."

Josie scooted the chair closer to the bed. "Here's what I believe. You and my dumbbell brother were out there in the woods that night, doing things you never should have been doing. Somehow the lantern was knocked over and you two knuckleheads were too busy to notice until it was almost too late for all of us!"

"What are you talking about? That's not true!"

"Really? Because I think that's *exactly* what happened." Josie was smirking, obviously proud of herself for having figured out the big mystery of the events that led up to the fire that night. Even though she was not present at the time. And none of what she had surmised was close to the truth.

"Josephine, I'm telling you, that is NOT what happened. It was him. He hit me on the head, and everything went dark."

"So, you would have me believe that Marcus, I mean, Mr. Berry gets the blame for you and Caleb messing around in the woods when you should have been doing chores?"

"I don't even…"

"Listen to me. I have my hands full taking care of this place and my siblings. The last thing I need is more on my plate to deal with. You go getting yourself into trouble and you are on your own."

`August shook her head. "Trouble?"

"Oh c'mon what do you take me for? You think I'm stupid don't you? Who do you think it was that cleaned you up after the fire? I don't think hitting your *head* on a rock would make a person bleed from…well, from…down there, do you?"

"Huh? I don't understand what you're saying." She pulled the covers back to see that she was wearing one of Josie's night gowns.

"That's right. Neither of you fools understand. Just a couple of stupid kids who don't know the first thing about what things can lead to. You better hope you ain't got yourself in a mess because I ain't raising another kid."

"A kid? I don't think we're talking about the same thing. I'm trying to tell you that he hit me over the head with something and I fell to the ground."

Again, Josie laughed, mocking her. "You really think that's true don't you? You think I ain't enough for him and he would rather have a scrawny lil waif like you?"

"I don't know what he was thinking but I'm telling you it was *him* that hit me over the head. I was heading to the barn to help Caleb with chores, and out of nowhere someone hit me. I heard his voice, Josie. It was him; I swear."

"Don't be telling anyone that nonsense story. Ya hear me? Deacon Berry is a good man who wouldn't want anything to do with trash like you! Just you and Caleb don't be doing whatever you were doing the night of the fire, ever again. Like I said, I've enough to do without more mouths to feed."

Nothing Josie was saying made a lick of sense to August. There was something she obviously wasn't understanding. Either *she* was confused, or Josie was downright cuckoo. Either way, they were not talking about the same thing. The pounding in her head was almost blinding and she longed for sleep. But, when she felt better, she would have this conversation again with Josie. This day was not the day. Josie was angrier than usual, and August couldn't see straight.

CHAPTER TWENTY-TWO

Life went back to normal at the farm, after the fire. Fortunately, no buildings were lost, only some of the trees between the house and the barn had been affected.

Though she tried many times, August never did find a suitable time to talk to Josie again about the events of that night like she had wanted. She decided it was just as well. Josie wasn't ever going to see "Saint Deacon" in the same dark sinister way that August did. She did ask Caleb about that night, though, without mentioning Deacon Berry's involvement.

Caleb also believed that August had tripped in the dark on her way to the barn that night, starting the fire accidently when she'd dropped the lantern. He

KARLA JORDAN

assumed she hit her head when she fell. He told her how grateful he was that she wasn't hurt badly and that the entire farm hadn't been burned to the ground. August knew he wasn't the type to look for anything more than what appeared on the surface of just about anything. His thought process was black and white just as his viewpoint of life was. She knew she'd be better off to leave the Deacon Berry business alone if she was going to continue to stay there at the farm.

August would never forget what he'd done though. She worried about what she'd say or do when she saw him again. She'd played out a hundred different scenarios in her head. She couldn't confront him in front of Caleb. Confront him in front of Josie? No. That was another bad idea. Keeping her distance when he was "visiting" the farm was the only plan that made sense.

Fortunately, she didn't have to worry about any of those things because he had not come back since the night of the fire. Not once. August wondered if Josie thought it weird that he hadn't come back to see her. August knew exactly why he hadn't but neither of the Donnelly's were going to believe her if she told them, and she figured it was best to let sleeping dogs lie.

Besides, there was something else she needed to talk to Josie about. Something besides the creepy Deacon. But, she had no idea how to go about talking to her about something serious. Josie wasn't exactly what anyone would call an approachable person. Other than the small talk they made when they had to, she and Josie didn't talk much about anything. August wished they had a better relationship, but they did not. Back when she had first come to the farm, she had hopes of them being close like sisters. It hadn't taken her long to see that it wasn't going to happen. Josie was full of resentment and anger and was either treating her like she didn't want her around or treating her like she was the hired help. Help that worked for free.

August learned that doing farm chores with Caleb was a lot less terrifying and frustrating than working inside. Every day after breakfast, she would quickly head out to the barn before she had to listen to a tirade from Josie about how she had to do everything herself. It was always the same song and dance from her, on loop, daily. The farm chores were hard and exhausting, but she didn't mind them. She worked hard right along with Caleb, and she slept good at night. In exchange, she was fed and had a roof over her head. Most of all, she was far from the terrible life she would have had had with Sal. If staying away from that life meant that she had to put up with Josie and her rantings, she could do it.

As she gathered eggs from the chicken coop, she practiced how she might approach Josie in the kitchen. It wasn't that she *wanted* to have a serious conversation with her specifically. She needed to talk to another woman, and Josie was the only possibility.

When August went inside, she could see that Josie was her usual closed off self. She sat at the kitchen table shelling beans and ignoring the fact that there was now someone else sitting beside her at the table.

"I know you don't like me much and that's okay. You don't have to. But you're the only other woman here and I need to talk to you about something important. Girl things."

Josie kept shelling beans and acted like she hadn't heard a word.

"Please Josie. I mean, Josephine. This is really something important."

She slammed her hand on the table. "So is getting supper ready! What do you want? And you better make it quick. As you can see, some of us have things that need to get done."

August didn't know the first thing about having a real conversation with this girl. And she sure wished she didn't need so badly to have one now.

"I suppose I should just get right to the point then. I haven't had my monthly in about three months."

Josie whipped her head around like it was on a swivel. "You what?"

"I said I haven't had my monthly in…"

"Never mind, you simpleton! I heard you the first time, I just can't believe what you said. I don't want to believe it and it damned well better not be true!"

She was no longer talking but screaming at August. The yelling woke Grace, who had been napping in the living room. Josie's voice kept rising higher and higher to be sure that she was heard over the baby's cries.

August didn't understand why Josie was so upset. It was *she* who had something wrong with her, not Josie.

"I don't know why you're so mad. It's not my fault if something is wrong inside me. I think I might need to see a doctor."

"A doctor? You think I'm sending you to see a doctor? Spending what little money there is around here to send YOU to a doctor?"

August was beginning to understand. It's about the money. It was always about the money with Josie. "But what if something's terribly wrong? Shouldn't I know? Shouldn't I have a doctor fix it?"

Josie laughed in a maniacal tone. "You idiot. There ain't no fixing what's wrong with you."

"How do *you* know? You're not a doctor."

"Ha! Don't need to be no doctor to know that you two are plain idiots. I knew something like this was going to happen. I just knew it!"

August was finding the conversation hard to follow. "Why am I an idiot? What did you know was going to happen? As usual, I don't understand what you are talking about."

"I'm sure you don't. If you did, you wouldn't be in this mess, now would you? You and my brother are both idiots. Shame on me for thinking he had half a brain in his damn fool head!"

"I'm not talking about Caleb. This is about ME. What aren't you understanding? I'm trying to tell you that something is WRONG with ME!"

"I heard you, loud and clear! What's wrong with you *is* his fault as much as it is yours. I knew I shouldn't have let you two spend so much time together. Probably all those days fishing down at the pond is what done it. Fishing huh? Yeah, right."

Josie paced the floor faster and madder than August had ever seen anyone walk before. August shook her head. "I still don't know why you're so mad. Something wrong with me has nothing to do with you."

Fire flew from Josie's eyes as she spun around to face August. "Oh no? Well just how in tarnation do you figure that? You and my dimwit brother couldn't control yourselves, acting like wild animals but it is ME that will suffer the consequences. *That's* what it's got to do with me."

"Caleb and I haven't done anything. Another mouth to feed? Wild animals? I'm lost."

"I can think of a zillion things I'd say you are but lost isn't one of them. I think ya pretend to be all innocent but ya don't know the first thing about being innocent."

"Why are you so angry? I am trying to understand what you're going on about but for the life of me, I just can't make head nor tails with any of it."

"Ya *cannot* be that dense. You just can't be. But I'm gonna go out on a limb and suppose you are. I'll spell it out real clear for you and if you listen close like, you just might get it. You. Aren't. Dying. There's nothing wrong with you that a doctor can fix. You are with child you dimwit. Is that clear enough for you to understand?"

August was silent.

"Cat got ya tongue all the sudden?" Josie chided.

August sat deep in thought trying to figure out how she could be carrying a child. After a few minutes, she looked at Josie.

"No. That makes no sense at all. No."

Josie had a plate in her hand which she fired into the cast iron sink and watched it shatter into tiny little pieces.

"No? You think all you have to do is say NO and it won't be true?"

August admitted to herself that she didn't know the first thing about what happens between a man and a woman when a baby is made. But whatever it took, she hadn't done. Not with Caleb. Not with anyone. Her entire understanding of birth had come from what she'd seen out in the barn between two goats. At the time, Caleb had explained that it meant they may have a baby goat or two in the spring after they mated. August certainly hadn't done *that* with anyone, so how could she possible be with child?

"I mean that no, I haven't done anything like that with Caleb or anyone. So NO I am not carrying a child."

Josie threw her hands into the air. Her face was red as red could be. August thought she looked demon like. "Girl, you don't have the brains God gave a caterpillar!"

August shook her head. She'd had enough of Josie and her hateful tirade. "Okay Josie. Yes, I said

JOSIE! I don't care if you want me to call you Josephine. I don't care about anything you want. I am sick and tired of being treated like I am nothing more than dirt that you scraped from bottom of your shoe. I knew I shouldn't have come to you! You are a mean, hateful brat who thinks that you're the only one in the entire world who has it rough. Go to hell Josie Donnelly! I'm done with you and your rotten attitude." she hollered.

"Done with *me*? Done with ME? Well, ain't' that just something. I knew I shouldn't have let you spend a single night here. I knew when I first saw you that you was nothing but trouble."

August's temper flared like she never even knew possible. "I've tried to be kind to you. I've done all that is asked of me and more. But I'm done now. I should have left the first night I came in here and you looked down your nose at me."

"How dare you come in here, to MY home and turn everything I've held together on a shoestring, upside down? You don't think feeding my family and now an illegitimate brat is too much to ask of a person?"

"I told you! I'm NOT having a baby!" she screamed.

Josie screamed right back. "Say it ain't true all you want. But you ARE! When a girl don't get her monthly for that long, it's exactly what it means!"

August stood in the middle of the kitchen shaking. Josie was screaming. Baby Grace was screaming, and she couldn't take it anymore. She covered her ears with her hands and started rocking back and forth. Josie was losing her mind and maybe she had too at that point.

"You and my brother don't share a brain between the two of you, I swear. How on earth God could see fit for a baby to be born to you two knuckleheads, I just can't imagine."

August couldn't take it anymore. The screaming in the room. The screaming in her head. There was no sense in trying to get through to Josie. She could plainly see that was never going to happen.

"I need to talk to Caleb. He's the only one around here with any sense." she said.

Josie picked up a mug and threw it in August's direction, just missing her head.

"You'll do no such thing. I want you out of here and I mean NOW! You go near my brother and so help me, girl. So help me."

August turned around to see Josie standing in the living room next to the fireplace. She had the rifle that hung over the mantle in her hands, and it was aimed straight at her head.

"Josie! What are you doing? Have you lost your mind?" August yelled and felt her entire body tremble. "Put that thing back on the wall. Don't be foolish!"

"For once, I'm not being foolish. For the first time since I laid eyes on you, I'm doing the right thing. I should have done it a long time ago. You get out of here and you head straight down that road you came in on. Don't you dare go running to my brother. Don't you dare!"

August felt every nerve in her body jumping

with fear. How had a simple conversation come to this? As she stared down the barrel of the rifle, she wished she were that bored little girl, with the father who didn't really want her, riding in the backseat from town to town while her Daddy sold illegal moonshine.

CHAPTER TWENTY-THREE

"Josie! Stop! What are you doing? Have you gone haywire or something?"

It was Caleb. He'd heard the screaming from the house on his way back from the barn and came running in to see what was going on. "Put that rifle down! Put it down this minute!" he yelled.

Josie wasn't listening to him any more than she had to August.

"I'll do no such thing. You tell your little girlfriend here to do as I say or I swear I'll fire it off, Caleb. I swear it."

Caleb had no idea what was going on or what had happened between the two of them to get his sister so riled up. Riled up enough to hold a gun on another person.

"I don't know what's going on in here and it don't much matter right now. Put that gun back on the wall and we'll sort it all out, okay?" he pleaded.

Josie laughed. "There's no sorting anything out now is there Caleb? I think the two of you should have thought about that about three months back. Three months ago when you were acting like wild animals down in the barn!"

"What? What are you talking about? We never..."

Her eyes grew wider, not you too? I thought that *you* at least would admit to the truth, but it goes to show you are both lying sacks of cow shit! You deserve each other. Don't let that door hit you on your backside either, Caleb. Turn around and head right on down that road with your little friend there!"

Caleb shook his head and roared, "Josephine Adelaide Donnelly, you put that rifle down this instant!"

He walked toward Josie with no apparent fear, acting more like a father than her younger brother. August was afraid for him because she could plainly see that there would be no reasoning with that girl.

"Caleb don't..." she screamed.

He turned toward the sound of August's voice. The ringing in her ears as the rifle went off was the loudest sound she'd ever heard. As if in slow motion, she saw the look of surprise in his eyes as his entire body slumped to the floor.

Josie had shot her brother in the back! August

screamed and Josie stood there with the rifle still held on August as she ran to Caleb. He wasn't moving and blood was beginning to pool around his body on the wooden floor.

"Don't! Josie demanded. "Do not go near him. Don't touch him. Don't even look at him or the same will be in store for you. Now git! I told you before and I mean it still. GET OUT of my house NOW!"

August shook her head. "But Caleb…"

"Never mind him, just go!" she screamed.

August looked at Josie with the rifle in her hands. She wasn't budging. She held it like she meant to use it again and August knew she would. She hadn't hesitated to shoot her own brother. It wouldn't phase her in the least to shoot her.

August looked over at Grace who was screaming from the living room. She felt bad leaving her with Josie, but she had no choice.

She didn't even bother to go into the room she'd slept in to grab her bag. August flew through the open kitchen door and ran. She ran until she had no more breath to breathe. She found herself once again fleeing like her life depended on it. Clearly it truly did.

A mile or so down the road, she stopped to catch her breath. She sat on a stump beside the dirt road and tried to understand all of what had just taken place.

Caleb was dead. Josie had held a rifle on him and pulled the trigger. She had killed her own brother. If only August hadn't chosen that day to talk to Josie. She should have known better. What was she thinking? Caleb was dead. It couldn't be real. The

183

entire thing could *not* have just happened. She didn't want it to be true. August held her head in her hands and cried hard from a deep, dark place, that she'd never known she had before. There seemed no end to the tears that raced down her cheeks.

She'd come to stay with the Donnelly's for a better life and Caleb had lost his life instead. The one person that she enjoyed spending time with, laughing with, learning with, was gone. She kept seeing his body as it lay on the floor, soaked in blood. And for what? Because Josie had lost her mind when August said she hadn't had her monthly? That was enough to set her off and put her in a state where she could do something like that? To her own brother?

She'd had it in her head that he and August had done something they shouldn't have been doing. She was convinced that they had made a baby together, but they hadn't. There was no telling her otherwise either. And now he was gone. What would become of Josie now? Or Grace? Without Caleb how were they going to manage to keep the farm running?

None of that was her concern anymore. She didn't even know how *she* was going to manage. How would she survive? Where would she go now that the only person that ever seemed to really care about her and treated her like he enjoyed being with her, was dead? She thought of those dimples when he smiled and his strong capable hands and his beautiful blonde hair blowing in the wind as they raced back to the house from the pond. And now he was gone. The life was draining from his body back at the farm, on the living room floor.

Her heart was broken. *Nothing* would ever matter to her again. Caleb was gone. He was no longer laughing, smiling, or breathing. He was gone and had taken her heart with him.

CHAPTER TWENTY-FOUR

It was almost dusk when a truck, driven by a woman carrying two girls in the back, pulled up beside her and stopped.

"Young lady, are you okay? Somewhere I can drop you off?"

August shook her head.

"There must be somewhere you need to be. It's almost dark and you can't stay out here in the middle of nowhere all alone, now can you?"

August shook her head again.

"Why don't you hop in the back with my girls? We have plenty of room at the house. You can stay with us for tonight. Tomorrow we can bring you wherever you want to go. How's that sound?"

THE ROAD TO MARIETTA

August declined with yet another shake of her head. She wanted to speak but every time she tried to talk, the tight knot in her throat triggered tears.

"I don't feel right leaving you out here like this. Go ahead, climb in the back with the girls. It'll be all right."

As if in auto mode, August stood and climbed into the back of the truck. She didn't know these people, but that didn't even seem to matter now. Nothing did. Her entire life had been a series of terrible things and most of them had come from trusting people she shouldn't have. What did she have to lose going with this woman and her children? She'd already lost everything she ever cared about.

The children tried to talk to August as they bounced around in the back of the truck, but she wasn't feeling that she wanted to or *could* speak. Her heart was broken, and she felt completely numb. The girls were older than Grace but younger than August. She knew they meant well but she had nothing left to give. Not even words.

Once at the woman's house, she introduced herself as Jane Goodman. Her children were Mary Ellen and Beth. Jane showed her to a room upstairs where she could stay for the night.

She explained that her husband, James, had gone East to Maine to find work at a quarry. Work had dried up since the depression hit hard in Indiana. A neighbor had relatives in Maine, who said the quarrying business was booming even though most of the economy was quickly going down the drain.

They'd been grateful for the opportunity for her husband to make money.

The next morning, after breakfast, Jane told the girls to play outside while she talked to August. She wanted to know about her situation and how she could help.

Mrs. Goodman seemed nice enough and August was grateful for the comfort of a meal and a bed. But there was no way on earth she could tell this woman anything about her "situation." How could she? Where would she even begin?

"Do you have family here?"

"No."

"Where were you going last night when I picked you up?"

"I don't know."

Jane fiddled with her teacup, arranging it repeatedly on the saucer. "Is there somewhere I could drive you?"

August shook her head.

"Has something happened to you? Is there something you want to talk about? I'm a good listener."

August simply shook her head.

"Has someone hurt you?"

August could hold back no more. The floodgates opened and she cried. She bawled like baby Grace had done when she had fallen into the pile of cow manure. Every time she tried to speak, she heard the rifle going off and saw Caleb's dying body lying on the floor.

She couldn't tell this woman about any of that. She

couldn't tell *anyone* about that. There was no way she would ever be able to get the words out, even if she wanted to. And she didn't want t. Not at that moment and maybe she never would.

Jane reached across the table and held August's hand without saying a word. When she spoke, she seemed slightly uncomfortable with what she was about to say. She shifted back and forth in the chair, as though she didn't really know how to start the conversation.

"This is none of my business and it may be nothing more than a wild guess. If I'm way off base, please forgive me. I'm wondering if there is a chance you may have found yourself in trouble? "In the family way" sort of trouble?"

August couldn't pull herself together to speak. She nodded her head and managed to whisper, "I think so."

Mrs. Goodman squeezed August's hand. "Okay then. Now the pieces are starting to come together. And the father? Is he around?"

August didn't know how to answer that. She only thought she was having a baby because that's what Josie kept saying. She knew nothing about a baby let alone a father. Still, she couldn't go into that whole story with Jane, so she just shook her head.

"Alright then, we'll see what we can do about your situation."

"*Do?*" August thought. She couldn't imagine what there was to *do*. She didn't even really believe there *was* a situation. There couldn't be. It was only Josie during her crazy tangent that had thought there was a situation. The only truth August knew for sure was the one that ended with Caleb lying on the floor. And there was nothing anyone could do about *that* situation.

"I know someone who can help you, I believe. I'll get the girls ready, and you can clean up if you like. When you're finished, I'll drive you across town to my friend."

August did as she was instructed without thinking about it. She got into the truck and Mrs. Goodman drove her to a large white house next to a church, with a tall steeple on the top.

"You sit tight for a minute. I'll go speak to my friend and when the time is right, I'll come back out to get you, okay?"

August nodded. Not speaking was so much easier and required much less effort. Her heart ached and her body felt lifeless. She didn't care who did what or where she went. The best part of her heart, her soul, was dead.

The girls played rhyming games in the back of the truck while August stared into an abyss of darkness, even though the sun was shining brightly.

Within minutes, Jane was back. "Come with me, Miss August. My friend is going to help you. There's a place for girls in your situation and you'll be safe there. Everything will be okay now. They know all about taking care of you and your baby there."

August nodded. She didn't care anymore if it *wasn't* okay. How much worse could it get than what she'd already been through? This woman had no way of knowing that nothing would ever be okay for her again. But August knew.

Jane opened the truck door and led her by the hand to a car that looked like the Model A that her father had driven. She hadn't known anyone but her father to drive a Model A, since it was the brand-new model, and most people couldn't afford such luxury in the tough times of the depression. Not that her father should have afforded it either.

"I've been asked to have you wait in the car. Shouldn't be but a minute, and my friend will take you where you need to go." She squeezed August's hand. "I wish you the best and I hope for wonderful things in this life for you, August. Take care of yourself young lady."

August watched as she and her children pulled out of the drive and soon were out of sight. She stared out the car window watching a grey squirrel run up and down a maple tree. She didn't notice a man walking toward the car and only saw him once he was already in the driver's seat, behind the wheel.

She turned her head to the sound of the closing door. Her mouth hung open and her eyes grew wide.

"You? You're Jane's friend?"

Deacon Berry smiled at her in that way that made her stomach heave. She held back the urge to throw up all over the inside of his car.

"Surprised to see me?"

August thought surprised was a bit of an understatement. Terrified was more like it.

CHAPTER TWENTY-FIVE

She scooted as close to the door and as far away from him, as she could. The man made her skin crawl. Being alone in a car with him did nothing to make her feel remotely safe. If only Jane knew what he was really like, she knew she wouldn't have gone to him for help.

He started the car and smiled at her in a way that made her entire body break out in goosebumps. As he drove, he had the nerve to try to make conversation with her. Conversation that she was not a bit interested in having. He asked about Josephine and her family. August had nothing to say. His ten-dollar suit and shiny black leather shoes didn't fool her. He was a monster who sought out young girls like

Josie and then preached a good old-fashioned heart felt sermon on Sundays.

"Go ahead and bring up Josie. You want to talk about that day I caught the two of you together? Go ahead. I dare you." She thought to herself.

She knew it was the last thing he wanted to talk about. Although he was talking plenty about "sins of the flesh" and going to hell for acting like a "heathen." Evidently he didn't think the scripture applied to him.

August so desperately wanted to tell him he was just as crazy as Josie. Wasn't he the same Deacon that she'd caught naked, lying on top of a young girl? Wasn't he the same man that hit her over the head that night of the fire? He was the absolute *last* person to be preaching to her about sinning or anything else, for that matter. But she kept all of that to herself. He wasn't worth her anger, and she didn't even care enough to tell him exactly how she felt. Nothing but Caleb, dead on the living room floor, mattered. Images of that day played on loop in her head, leaving no room for thoughts of anything else.

The overpowering scent of cheap cologne filled the car making August feel nauseous. The Deacon was blabbering on about something or another and she was doing her best to ignore him. Until she couldn't.

"And then, imagine my luck when I opened my door this morning to Mrs. Goodman who had quite the tale about the homeless little girl she'd found beside the road. A poor soul who had found herself in the family way and just a child herself. Poor little thing with such a lovely name of August."

She glared at him long enough to roll her eyes and be sure that he'd seen her doing so.

"And I thought to myself, "Imagine that. Just imagine that. The good fortune the Lord has given me today." He laughed like a hyena.

August ignored him and kept looking out the window at the houses and passing trees.

"We're almost there now. Just over the state line. Should be far enough, I would think."

August snapped her head around toward him. "Far enough? Far enough for what?"

He laughed again sending a cold chill up her spine. "Far enough for no one to care about anything you might feel you want to run your naughty little trap about."

She didn't care what he was going on about. She didn't want to talk, especially to him. She didn't know what he meant by the comments, and she really didn't care. When they got to where they were going, he would drop her off and he would leave and she had zero intentions of ever seeing that man, the devil in disguise Deacon, ever again.

Fortunately, they drove in silence for the rest of the ride until they pulled up to a large square, brick building with a flat roof. The grounds were beautifully manicured with flowers growing in beds and under the trees in a circular pattern. August had never seen any place quite as beautiful.

The Deacon turned the car off but made no attempt to get out. When August reached for the door handle, he spoke in a loud, stern voice. "Wait just a minute.

I need to be sure you understand something clearly before you go."

August kept her hand on the door, but she turned her head to face him.

"Don't be getting any ideas about telling these people, or anyone, ever. Do you understand me?"

August was confused. "Tell anyone? Tell anyone what?"

He grinned in that way that made her feel dirty. "That's right. That's what you continue to do. No one needs to know anything about what we did. You hear?"

"I hear you. I just don't have any idea what you're talking about and honestly I don't care. Just let me out of this car!"

The Deacon grinned wide, and August cringed. "Oh, come now, you remember the night of the fire. You can't tell me you didn't enjoy every second of it as much as I did. You forget, I *saw* how much you liked it."

August felt sick again. "What? I don't even remember the night of the fire. I hit my head when I tripped over a rock or something."

"A rock? Weren't no rock little girl. It was a big ole heavy branch right upside your head. I had to do something to stop you from running away, now didn't I?"

August shook her head. "I think you're as crazy as your girlfriend, Josephine. You do remember her don't you? I'm sure you do, you nasty pervert."

She pulled at the door latch trying to get out and run away as fast and as far as she could. Deacon Berry reached across the car in front of her and put his hand over hers.

"Say what you want to *me*, but don't you dare tell another living soul about you and me and the fun we had. If you do, I'll track you down and you'll be sorry. I swear I will make you sorry you were ever born."

August squinted her eyes as she stared at him eye to eye. "It wasn't me you did disgusting things with. If you remember right, you creep, it was ME who caught you with Josie. I wonder how your wife and the high and mighty church people would like to know about that?"

He scowled at her and let go of the door handle and backhanded her hard across the face.

"Josie wasn't half the wildcat you were, I'll give ya that. Course I didn't account on you being dumb enough to get pregnant. I should have known better."

August fought the tears as she tried to understand what he was saying. She and the Deacon? They'd done what she saw him and Josie doing? There was no way that could be true. It just couldn't.

"If you are telling the truth, which I doubt, you are more of a disgusting pig than I thought. I was unconscious, and you took advantage of me?"

He laughed out loud. "You don't fool me none girl. Your eyes might have been closed but I could see how much you were enjoying every minute just the same as me."

August felt like she was going to be sick. She could feel her breakfast begin to make its way out of her stomach and rise into her mouth. Everything was closing in on her. She was dizzy, sweating, and scared half to death. She needed to get away from this man. She pulled the latch, opened the car door, and threw herself onto the ground. When she had finished throwing up, she laid on the cool green grass and cried. She hugged her knees and watched the car drive off, thankful that the monster had left.

"God, if you are real and if you can hear me, I need to know why? Why was I born? Why was I never wanted? Why did my Daddy hate me so much? Why did my Mama have to die? Why did you send me to Sal? Why oh, God, why did Caleb have to die? And most of all, how could you ever let a creep like Deacon Berry do this to me? I just don't understand. I don't understand." she cried.

Just then, a woman in a black dress with a black cloth head covering, reached for her. August jumped at the touch and scooted across the grass on her behind.

"No! Don't touch me! No one ever touch me again! Ever!" she screamed at the top of her lungs repeatedly until the bright sunshine filled day turned to dark in seconds.

When she awoke sometime later, she was greeted by the woman she'd seen outside earlier. August was in a room with five other beds. Everything was white. The walls were white. The floors were white. The bedding was white. Even the night dress she was wearing was white.

"Where am I?" she whispered.

"My name is Sister Agatha, and you are at the Rising

Saint Home for Girls. It's a home for unwed mothers. You'll be safe here with me and the other sisters. And, of course there are plenty of other girls here in the same situation as yourself."

"Unwed mothers?" August murmured.

And then the details of what Deacon Berry had told her came flooding back into her mind. And she cried. She mourned for the life she never had. She mourned for the life that had been taken when Josie shot Caleb. She mourned for the life that was alive inside of her. She longed to feel Rosa's arms around her telling her that everything would be okay with a cup of tea and a plate of Snickerdoodles.

But that wasn't going to happen. It couldn't. Those days, along with her childhood and innocence, were long gone. They could never come back.

CHAPTER TWENTY-SIX

March 27, 1931

I've given up talking. I don't want to speak ever again. Using my voice hasn't served me or done any good, so I have stopped using it. You are the only one I want to talk to anyway. Talking requires too much energy and untangling of thoughts that are all jumbled up in my head. There's nothing in there that anyone would want to hear anyway. Too much sadness.

You are the only one I care to know how I feel about anything, and so I will continue to not speak to anyone around me, except for you.

You are growing inside of me now, even as I write. This place isn't so bad. The nuns are nice to me and none of the girls here seem to mind it either. Even they have been nice to me, but I decided after what happened to a good friend of mine, that I don't want to be friends with anyone, even though the girls do try to befriend me. It hurts too much to lose someone you care about, so I figure I'll just stick to myself. And of course, I have you so I'm not alone now and I never will be again.

The doctor here says you are almost eight months old inside of my tummy. Sometimes you kick a lot in there and even wake me up at night. But I don't mind a bit.

I wonder what you look like sometimes when I can't sleep. I wonder if you have the same jet-black hair as my mama and me. I wonder so much about you. Can you hear me when I talk to you in my mind? Do you like it when I hum that lullaby? I sang it to another baby I knew once and she always liked it, so I hope you do too. Do your tiny little hands and feet look like mine, I wonder. I think about you every minute of every day. I hope that you feel happy and safe inside my tummy. I want so badly for you to always know what happiness and contentment feel like. I, myself, never knew much about either of those things but I want you to. I don't want you to ever doubt, not for one second, that you are loved, because you are.

I'll tell you the truth about something, but only you. When I first came here, to the Rising Saint House for Girls, I wasn't even sure I wanted to be alive anymore. Nothing had ever gone as I wished or wanted it to, so I had all but given up. Now, when the doctor showed me a picture in a book, of what you might look like inside of me as you grow, something wonderful happened. I realized that I wasn't alone. You, my baby, have given me a reason to want to wake up every morning. A reason to take care of myself like I should.

I've come to look forward to seeing the doctor now. He tells me about how big you should be at each visit. Although I don't know what giving birth to you will be like (I've heard some of the girls talk about how painful it is) but I don't care. When it's all over, I will see your tiny little face and hold you to my heart. You will be mine to love and care for. I can't wait to see your tiny little eyes, nose, mouth, and ears. I promise I will take good care of you and give you a good life. A life so much better than the one I was given.

March 28, 1931

I saw the doctor again today. He told me that you have hair and tiny little toenails and fingernails now. Before today, I was seeing you in my mind as a little doll. I never thought about things like fingernails. I still don't speak to anyone, but I've realized that I do smile often now. I smile because I know that I am the proud mother of a beautiful baby girl or boy.

April 1, 1931

Veronica, the girl in the bed next to mine, went into

labor today. That's what it's called when a mother starts to give birth to a baby. The other girls say that sometimes a baby comes quick and sometimes labor is days long with much pain. I'd say Veronica had one of those painful labors because she woke us all up in the middle of the night screaming and writhing.

The sisters took her into the labor ward hours ago and she hasn't come back yet. Everyone is wondering if she has had her baby and if she's okay. She's been nice to me since I came here, so I hope she is well.

April 2, 1931

Today Molly, who was across the room from me for the past few months went into labor. She wasn't screaming in pain like Veronica did when she had her labor. Veronica stood up from her bed where she had been reading a book and suddenly there was a warm pool of water on the floor. Sister Agatha said that Molly's water had broken. That's another thing that happens when it's time to give birth. Oh, and Veronica didn't come back either. None of us are sure why or where either of them went. Sister Agatha keeps telling the girls who ask, "All in good time, girls. All in good time." Whatever that means.

April 4, 1931

Today I went for a long walk outside. It was a beautiful day with all the flowers around. I think you like Daisies. You sure kicked up a storm when I bent over to pick one. Maybe I'll call you "Daisy." I guess I should wait to decide that until I see you. You could be a boy. Either way, it won't matter what you are. If you are a boy, I will love you. If you are a girl, I will love you. I will just have loads and loads of love for you.

April 5, 1931

The room is emptying out around me. It's only been a few days since Molly had her baby and now Gillian is in labor. She was having a nap when her pains started this afternoon. When the other girls asked Sister Agatha if the baby had come yet, she said "It'll come in God's time and not until." I hope he doesn't make me wait much longer to see you my sweet, sweet baby.

April 7, 1931

    I don't feel good today. I've spent most of the day in bed. The sisters said I have a "bug" of some sort. Whatever it is, I'm very tired and the pain in my head is barely tolerable. You've been still today too, and I sure am hoping that you feel better than I do at this moment.

April 9, 1931

    The last time I wrote to you, I wasn't feeling well, but that passed after a couple of days. I feel better now.

    There's something wrong with one of the girls. The doctor said she should have given birth to her baby by now, but she hasn't even begun her labor. The doctor is coming for her soon to do something that will help her baby be born. I don't know what they do about that. Neither does Susan. She looks like she's worried and scared. I keep hearing her talk to God and prays that nothing is wrong with her baby.

    I can't even imagine how scared I'd be if that were me. If something were to happen to you, I just can't imagine. But it won't. I've never wanted anything more in my entire life than to be your mother. I love you and I know you must feel that from where you are. I hope you do. Hopefully, you will be born soon, and I can smother your face with a million kisses.

April 11, 1931

I have two new roommates. They arrived earlier today. Amy and Sara Jane. They aren't as big as a house yet, like your Mama is, but they will be in a few months. They talk a lot, and the room is hardly ever quiet when they are both in it. I still haven't spoken. I'm saving up all my words for you.

April 12, 1931

You sure have been kicking a bunch today. You move around in there so often now. Sister Agatha says you have "dropped." I was worried about that, and I think she could see it on my face. She told me it was a perfectly natural part of giving birth. She says it shouldn't be much longer until my labor starts. That makes me happy and excited.

I go for walks almost every day now. It feels good on my back and my hips when I walk. Also, I'm quite sure you like it outside too. Your little feet kick right up into my ribs when I'm walking. I think that means you're happy to take walks with me. Once you are born, I promise to take you for walks every single day if you want me to.

I'll see you soon my sweet baby.

April 15, 1931

It's been three days since I last wrote. This morning you woke me up kicking so much that I just couldn't get comfortable lying down. A few minutes later, I stood up and saw that my water had broken. I started having cramps in my belly but those have slowed down now. The doctor said not to worry. He said you will be moving toward your birth soon. I sure hope so. I can't wait to meet you.

April 30, 1931

My dear, dear child. It's been two weeks since I last wrote. You are no longer growing or kicking inside of me. You arrived out into the world in the middle of the night on April 16, 1931.

I haven't written because I haven't been able to find the words. I'm not sure I can still, but I feel I should. I feel that one day you may need to know. I don't even know if that's possible really. But just in case, I'm going to tell you some things.

I'm sorry to tell you that the day you were born, you were taken from me. I held you for the briefest of minutes before one of the sisters took you from me. I thought they'd return you to me after cleaning you up. They did not.

I never knew until that moment, that they never had any intention of letting me be your mother. This is how it goes for all the girls here; I now know.

It's a home for unwed mothers. Once the girls give birth, the babies are taken and given to couples who want to adopt a child. All of us are under the age of eighteen here, so the law says we are unable to keep our babies.

For six months, I was here, and I never once knew that. If I had, I would have run away and never looked back. It honestly never dawned on me that this is why the girls never came back to the room after going into labor. They never came back at all.

The minute they took you away from me, my heart broke into a million tiny pieces. It is still broken. It will always be broken. I gave up not talking when they would not return you. I screamed. I begged. I cried. And still, they would not bring you back to me. I don't even know where you are because they won't tell me that either. I will try to find you for the rest of my life.

I never want you to think that I didn't want or love you because I did. You were the only person I have ever loved like that, and I never will love anyone like that again. Ever. I did name you "Daisy," but the home said your new family will give you the name they choose. I have no idea what name they have given you, but you will always be my Daisy.

For the rest of my life, there will be a hole in my heart for the part of me that was taken. Someone else may hear you call them "Mommy" but only I will ever know the feeling of you growing inside of me or feeling your heartbeat in time with my own. I loved every second of carrying you in my belly. I loved feeling you grow and I'm grateful for the chance to hold you in my arms. Even if it was for a brief time.

Sister Agatha has been good to me and has taken me under her wing. All the other girls have families to go back home to, but I do not. She has asked me to stay and help in the kitchen until I am old enough to live on my own and find work that pays money. So this is where I'll be for a few more years. It's hard to stay here knowing that this place is where I lost my baby girl but it's all I have. I am grateful to Sister Agatha for helping me out but not a single day goes by that I don't wish I could be with you. I want you to know that as soon as I'm old enough to leave here and earn my own money, I'll pay someone to help me find you. A detective person or someone like that. I don't care how much it costs; I will save every penny I earn, to try to find you. Sister Agatha says the pain will heal in time but she's wrong. I know it never will. I know she's trying to be kind, but she doesn't know the pain of having you taken from my arms, never to be returned.

This is the last time I will write because it just hurts too much. I don't know that you will ever read any of my ramblings anyway.

Please know that my heart misses you every second of every single day. A mother's love never dies, and I now know this about my own mother's love also. Thank you for showing me that.

I pray that I find you one day and that somehow you will know that I am your mother.

Until then, I pray that you are in a good, kind, loving home. I hope that you will be treated well and always loved. I will feel your presence with me every single day for the rest of my life.

Until we meet again dear girl. Forget me not, Daisy.

Your loving mother,

August Violet Finnegan

CHAPTER TWENTY-SEVEN

August 8, 1971
Allison Treadway
245 Angelo Drive.
Cleveland, OH 77778

Dear Ms. Treadway,

Enclosed please find a newspaper clipping along with a personal diary. Both previously belonged to the woman that is believed to be your biological mother. Her name was August Violet Finnegan.

The town of Marietta, Ohio contacted me when Ms. Finnegan passed. I did some searching and saw that she gave birth to a baby girl on April 16, 1931, at the Rising Saint Home for Girls. The home has since closed but the records are still available in archives. There was only one baby girl born at the Home on that date. I further noted that your parents received a newborn girl on the same date from said Home. I searched your name and was fortunate to find your name listed as an Ohio resident.

Please contact me at my office at your earliest convenience as I believe you to be the child she gave birth to. Once this is established for certain, I have financial documents to go over with you, as well as personal items that need to be signed for. We will go through all details at that meeting. Please also find the newspaper announcement that gives the details for the graveside service that will take place next week on August 15, 1971, should you wish to attend.

Sincerely,

Eugene Akers
Attorney at Law

****

Allison sat in the gazebo of her home with a fresh cup of coffee, surrounded by a stack of diaries that belonged to her biological mother. She felt like she'd been given priceless treasures when the attorney had given her the yellowed, tattered books containing the thoughts of a woman she'd always wondered about. She knew she was fortunate to have an opportunity to peek into the life of the woman who had brought her into the world. Allison knew it was a gift that many adopted children never are afforded.

As excited as she was to read each page, there

was also a feeling of guilt tugging at her heart. As though reading someone's deepest thoughts and feelings, was somehow infringing on their privacy. August *did* write them for her however, so she would cherish every word.

There was also a life insurance policy in the amount of $25,000 left to her daughter, her only family, though she had no idea if her child could be found at the time of her death. Fortunately, the attorney had located Allison quickly and was able to release the funds and personal items. He was also setting up an education fund to help unwed mothers called The August Finnegan Trust. August was thrifty and led a simple life. She had managed to save a small, yet tidy, sum that one day would be used to help young mothers work toward an education and live a better life. The Trust was August's wish and Allison was proud to watch it take shape.

Reading through the diary entries, Allison quickly came to understand that August was like no other person she had ever met. She'd worked as a telephone operator in Marietta, Ohio when she was old enough to leave The Rising Saint Home and continued to work there until she passed away. Other than the necessities such as rent, utilities and the most modest of food expenses, the woman had saved up every dime to give to a daughter that she'd never had a chance to meet. Allison also was given a box of needlework linens that August had sewn by hand. She would cherish them forever.

August had no way of knowing that her

daughter had been adopted and raised by a great family. Not once did Allison ever feel not loved by them. And, though she never knew her biological mother, she always felt a connection to her. She'd always felt like there had to be a good reason for her mother to give her up to another family. Never in her wildest dreams though could Allison have ever imagined the true story of how that came to be or how it was that she had come to be in existence.

Her heart ached for the child that August was and for all the suffering that she had to go through in her short life. It wasn't fair that some people had it all and some, like her mother, had done all the right things and still never managed to find the happiness they deserved. Something that Allison realized she had taken for granted as a child and even as an adult. But she wouldn't ever again. Not after learning how much a thirteen-year-old girl had gone through in life yet dedicated her life to an infant she'd never had the pleasure of raising as her own. No, going forward, Allison was going to look at the world in a different light. In a light that August would be proud of. Not that her life had ever been anything to be ashamed of, because it was not. She'd done well. She had a lovely home, a respectable job working in marketing and a supportive and loving family.

However, as she read the handwritten scrawls on the pages, it had become apparent to her that giving back was something she might not have embraced as much as she should have. She would spend the rest of her life being more like the woman who brought her into this world. She would help those in need more. She would keep the Trust running and fully funded for as long as she lived. If she could help even one girl who found themselves in the position that her mother had at such an immature age, she would feel proud of that.

She hoped that somewhere in the universe, August Violet Finnegan was smiling. Allison felt sure this was the case. She would devote her life going forward to making sure that her mother kept smiling, wherever she was.

Morningside Cemetery
Cleveland, Ohio

Allison Treadway stood beside the grave of a mother she never knew. It was a simple granite headstone that she had chosen for August. She was the only attendee besides the minister.

After the simple service, she laid a bouquet of freshly picked daisies on the wooden casket and said, "Thank you for giving me life. I hope you can see me from where you are and know that I am happy. I wish

I could have known you. I know I would have loved you."

A single tear ran down her cheek as she turned to leave.

****

In the distance, two people stood in the shadows of a large, shady Elm tree. "Are you ready to go?" she whispered.

He wiped a tear from his eye, hoping that she didn't see. "I suppose I am, Grace. Thank you for bringing me here today. She didn't know I was here, but I know. It means a lot to me to be able to give her that."

She smiled and took him by the arm. "I was glad to do it and I hope it also brings you some peace, Caleb."

He nodded. "It does indeed. She is free now and with the angels where she always belonged. C'mon sis, let's go home."

THE END?

THE ROAD TO MARIETTA

KARLA JORDAN

THE ROAD TO MARIETTA

ABOUT THE AUTHOR

Karla Jordan

Karla is also the author of "Cartwheels In The Dark" her debut novel published in December of 2021 on Amazon.

She lives in Maine, where she shares a life with her husband, their two dogs and their cat. When she's not writing, she enjoys spending time with family and friends, gardening, and baking.

If you liked this book, please consider going to Amazon, Facebook, Instagram, Twitter, Goodreads, Bookbub or anywhere you give your book reviews and let me (and others looking for an enjoyable read) know what you think.

If you have not signed up for my newsletter and would like to, you can find the sign up on my webpage:

karlawjordan.com

Also, if you are not a social media friend, why not? I love to hear from readers.
 Facebook: Karla Jordan Author
Instagram: KarlaJordan56
Twitter: @Karla W Jordan

29512713R00136